David And Bath Sheba

To order additional copies, please contact us.
BookSurge, LLC
www.booksurge.com
1-866-308-6235
orders@booksurge.com

AIDA
BODE

DAVID AND BATH SHEBA

2005

David And Bath Sheba

To: My late mother Emilia Karanxha, the person that educated my spirit with goodness and love, with willingness and work, with determination and desire for the future.

To: The memory of my grandfather Petro Nani, the person who taught me how to find beauty in every story, real or tale. In his voice I captured the truthfulness of tales and the dreams of reality.
To: My father Llambro Karanxha, the person who taught me how to find goodness within myself and make that goodness success, make it part of my life.

To: My family: My brothers, grandmothers, great-grandmothers, all the people who blessed my life with their every breath and laughter, with every cry and criticism, with every support and love.

If I know life and its ways, this knowledge is because of the abundance of love that I have been given from this family where I was born and raised. I am more than blessed, I am preferred by GOD!
To: The most wonderful love that I live: My husband, my daughter, my son and my mother in law.

I t was the first time since the kingdom was given to him that he was spending the first days of the New Year in the palace. Everywhere people had celebrated the biggest event of the year. It was the eternal commandment from God since He had liberated them from the Egyptians that they should commemorate Passover, their salvation. It truly was one of the most beautiful moments of the year to think of God's greatness, goodness and faithfulness toward Israel, but it also was one of the most difficult. In the beginning of every New Year, the king and his army were to fight against the enemies of the land that God had promised to them, but this year, something strange had kept him in the palace.

He had found himself in midst of a solitude that had given him a desire to meditate on what had happened. The passing year had been filled with events that had brought victory, longings, promises kept and, above all, goodness from God, whom he adored with all his power and might.

***

He was raised surrounded by the love of his parents and the romps of his brothers at a time when only love and grace could guard family and life. The people were under the yoke of their occupier, but not him and the spirit of his family. They were free in God of Israel, whom they worshiped, and awaited salvation from. Everyday, he would lean on his mother's lap and with his curious eyes would wait to hear a story of deliverance from her. He would amaze himself at the miracles that his people had lived throughout the years with God, and caught in the passion of the Lord, he would ask the person who he thought knew everything: "Mom, why are we suffering now; don't people remember God's works anymore?" She would stroke his curly hair and with a warm voice would say: "My son, people are weak, they are impatient, they forget goodness and they follow their own ways when they don't understand. So is with our people; we have forgotten in our weakness. Keep your heart in the Lord's will and you will always find grace and goodness in His ways."

He would think of his mother ... that incredible being, fragile as he, strong like nothing else, undressed from life when near him, deep and endless in love toward the fruit of her womb. She would lose herself in his little bright eyes, which told her how much he loved her, and she would think of the time when she had given love unconditionally, without any doubts. In his deep glittery eyes, she would marvel herself, and she would bless that miracle that God Himself had given her. He was her beloved son. He was David.

He was her youngest son, but she regarded him as her firstborn. In her dreams and heart's desires, she saw her son's ways and knew that David was the pride of her hopes, in her soul she was the mother of the king, the mother of the victorious, and the mother of the one who was after God's own heart. Delighting in this truth and humble in grace, she cherished... cherished his breathing, his little movements, cherished the looks in his eyes, cherished his curly hair that fell like little honeysuckle on his sweet face. She cherished him as she tried to stop time, to spend eternity with her little boy, who grew each day before her eyes. And he, he would follow every movement of her's that would make the brightness in his eyes radiate, and smile of love. He would move his little hands to imitate her caresses and he would play with the goodness of her spirit. He would see himself in her eyes and would know he was their apple; he was their mirror of love, their splendor of dreams; he was her heart's humility. He learned in her embrace that only God has such endless arms of warmth. He heard in her voice the sound of music, found poetry in her words, and met with love in her face. In her spirit he lived life, and was grateful that she was given to him. He, David, the man after God's own heart, saw his future in the blessings and desires of his mother's heart.

***

As he was wandering on the roof of his palace, he lifted up his eyes to the sky and felt mesmerized at the richness of stars that adorned the infinite expanse. Powerless to move his lips, he whispered under his breath: "O, my loving Lord! Isn't it marvelous that you have created such a magnificent world for us humans who are only its dust? Here I am standing stunned before all this and...I know this isn't where I should be now. I should have gone and lead my army in the battlefield. Forgive me for my disobedience, and please grant victory to your children!" A falling star got his attention, and he followed it with his eyes tearful of shame. He thought he was that star, far from the stream of light, falling in loneliness.

***

He remembered Saul, and his fall. Saul had met with David in peace, but had persecuted him like an enemy. He had been a rival for Saul, always a step ahead of him, and Saul always wanted to get in front.

But the persecution was over now, and with it, the life of the persecutor. However, he felt pain and sadness for his loss. Saul, the king, had been his enemy from the moment that he had been his friend and comforter. David had wept for the loss of the king, he had never considered him a bad man, and always respected him to the end of his life. He had loved his king and had always seen in him God's chosen one. He remembered when the king made him a soldier of his army and he was filled once more with love and respect for that man that persecuted him, but that now was no more.

***

He was but a youth, who didn't know fighting with arms and human enemies, but his spirit was full of fire and passion for justice and freedom. It was a difficult time, his brothers were all in service to the king's army, and they were fighting against the Philistines. David was the only one left home caring for his father's sheep. Time after time he would visit his brothers and would bring them food or clothing, and he would encourage them with his spirit for victory in their battles. But his faith and desires alone were not enough for fighters like his brothers who had lost their hopes and strengths in a war where the enemy was more selfish than they were meek, more idolatrous than they were godly, more proud than they were humble, more coward than they were brave. A Philistine, with the body of a giant and the voice of a tyrant, had come out in the middle of the battlefield and was showing how swollen with pride he was inside his steel armor. None of the children of Israel would dare to even look at this blaring pretentious who with his big sized body, and his hoarse voice had won a battle that hadn't even began. As David heard his voice, he was caught in his passion and was driven by his faith in God, and asked his brothers to take him before the king. They knew David well, they knew he was determined in his requests and achieved his goals, so they didn't try to stop him, hoping that no matter what he would offer, the king would refuse him because of his young age.

As they were walking to the king's tent, David started thinking of the times he had protected his father's sheep from the beasts of the field. He would think of the words that he would say to the king, he would show him his faith in God, that faith that had never let him down, in caring for his father's herd. When they got to the tent, the guards stopped them, questioned them, and then allowed them to get in. One of the brothers approached the king, who was in despair and disappointment:

"My lord and my king, our brother David, who has come here today to visit us, desires to offer you his service, for which my brothers and I disagree. "

David followed closely all the king's movements, and was astonished at this man's greatness, who was chosen by God to be the leader of Israel, but now was keeping his head low and his hand on his chin. He lifted up his eyes and started talking slowly:

"My son, son of my saddened hours, what has brought you here in this black day for my army? I know you play the harp so well; your songs are my peace, but what more can you do to save the honor of my fighters? Aren't these valiant soldiers you see today set back by the yelling of this uncircumcised, the same soldiers that have fought by my side in battles? Don't they know the zeal of fight and the way to victory? My son how can you come to me and what can you offer that will make these warriors and this army get on its feet again?"

His eyes were down with fatigue and his voice was drowned in the anguish of a battle that was fiercer than any other before. He had spent hours praying to God to give him this tyrant, but nobody, not even him, dared to face and fight him.

"My king and my lord, I don't come to you in conceit, I don't come to you in arrogance, otherwise I wouldn't be more than this Philistine who's blaspheming the name of our God. I have come to tell you that God keeps His promises. I have not fought with people, but I have fought beasts, and I know I don't possess any strength other than what God gives me when I follow his promise. My father's sheep are my promise, and not one of them have I lost, because God has been their guard. He has taught me how to wrestle the beasts, keep safe what is mine, and protect those gifts He has given me. I fear, but more than that I trust, more than fear I have God's desire for this battle, and I know it is ours. I ask your blessing so that I may go out and conquer this fool dressed in iron. And if you don't trust in God, just trust this, you will lose nothing, this battle has to start, give me the blessing to be the one to start it."

Saul didn't answer. He fixed his eyes on David's body and was astounded at his faith and the strength of his spirit. He knew David, he was his comforter, and now he was offering him salvation, he was offering his life.

This youth had a heart full of melody and words of songs that made every evil flee, every difficulty ease, every darkness light, every obstacle solution, every enemy friend, and every hate love. This youth was showing the king that he wasn't scared of fear, or shy of boldness, he was ready to take God and raid toward anything that didn't let him prosper. Looking at his invincible eyes, his soul dressed with courage, Saul thought to himself: "Who am I to stop what God wants to do with this young man? He spoke to us, but we didn't listen; now He comes to us with ears that hear, and a heart that obeys, who am I not let Him do what He has to do?"

"Go my son, and bring us the victory that God has promised you!"

These were his words, his blessing, and his acceptance. He let David go out in the field and watched him wearing nothing but his faith, approaching the Philistine fearlessly, holding a sling in his hand, and carrying five stones in his bag. God delivered the giant in his hands, and he put him down with a sling shot; a sling shot that made the field roar with shouts of victory, a sling shot that gave glory to God, whom he adored. David would never forget this moment that made him man and partaker in his peoples' fight, a people who were in anguish for freedom and God's Word.

**

He would think of how Saul was chosen, and how God made him the first king of Israel, the first person to be crowned for the glory of God, enthroned for His honor. Saul was zealous for the people and passionate for justice. A passion that cost him everything that God had given him, but David never judged his king, he followed him in battles from that day that he blessed him, until the day that he lost his life on mountain Gilboa. Suffocated in loss and lamentation, David cursed that mountain and hated that battlefield where an anointed life had ended, he remembered Saul's bravery and Jonathan's love, he cried out to God for their lives and he mourned their death. Nothing would comfort his soul, the loss of the king, was the loss of Israel's pride, and Jonathan's loss was the loss of a part of his heart. He couldn't find a lap to slam his grief, other than the dust of the earth, and he couldn't mourn other than with ashes, with his torn spirit and his heart in pieces, he and all people lamented the fall of Israel's eagle.

Now he carried on his shoulders Saul's burden, his boldness and passion, he carried Jonathan's love, and an anointing that would be his and his descendants'. He stood before the Lord to take what Saul had left behind to rise it up on high from where it had fallen. Now he was king to walk in humility and obedience, he was king to honor the one before him, he was king to glorify the God that made him king.

**

As he was walking slowly, his steps fell softly on the tiles of the roof. He was now standing in front of his officers' palace. The children's noises had died with the day, and the moon lightened the darkness inside the building. Again his thoughts took him into the past where he would find joy and delight. He remembered when Saul gave him his daughter in marriage. She was his price, was his dowry, she was his first desire toward woman, was the first to have given him complete love. Where did all that love go, where did her passion vanish? She despised him in his moment of glory; she abased him in his love for the Lord.

**

He was king of all Israel, but there was one thing that was far from his heart: the Ark of the Covenant that was in Baale of Judea. Surrounded by chosen men of Israel he went to bring the Ark in the City of David. He was filled with the joy of God's glory, and the pride of a people, whose leader and savior was God himself. The Ark was filled with holiness and covered by an untouched surface that would make every man tremble. They placed the Ark on a cart of cattle and lead the way to the City of David singing and dancing. The stones on the road were rejoicing with their song, and the day shined itself with the happiness of this glorious moment, the harps, and the psalteries chimed crystal sounds praising the Name of the Lord, the cymbals, and the drums made everything dance from joy. The cattle looked like they were dancing, too. They were all walking toward the city filled with this love and happiness, making noise, and dancing for the Lord, but for one moment it seemed like the cattle shook the Ark, and one of the men near took a hold of it. He shuddered and fell down, as if he was struck by a lightning. David felt a trembling all over his body, and ran in sadness toward the man. Uzzah was lying on the ground holding a frozen pain on his face that David had never seen before. Holding out his hand, he closed his eyes that were saying: "I'm leaving because I sinned!" David was hurt from this sudden death, and filled with a fear he had never experienced before he asked himself: "How can the Ark of the Covenant come to me? The Lord is untouchable, and...and I, I am so weak... we were rejoicing, and one mistake, one transgression, one desire to touch something that is not ours, brought us death."

He ordered for the cattle to be directed to another town, but he returned to his city troubled that once again he was far from the thing he loved most: The Ark of the Covenant.

After some time he heard that the town where the Ark was, was living in fullness and bounty. David understood that God is good toward those who are humble so he sent for the Ark to be brought once again into the City of David, and sacrificed oxen, and fatlings. He danced like never before. Dressed in a linen robe he humbled himself in front of all his servants, and gave praise to God uncovering his body and spirit. As he was rejoicing, he noticed the one that had loved and protected him, his first wife, looking at him with contempt and disdain.

The celebration was over and his heart was filled with the events of that day, which had made him more than a king. He was the chosen of his people. As he was going to share his joy with his family, she came before him with a face where bitterness and irony had made their dwelling. She was like a golden dish filled with poison, she walked with beauty that was fading from the sorrows of the past, and she neared like a ghost that was hoping for a resurrection that was never promised. He could see in her eyes the rave of her father and Jonathan's pure love. He could see the persecution of hate, and the support of affection, he could see his fight with the enemy, and the first love that she had given him. He could see the betrayal that had made her the woman of another man.

"You were really honorable today, o King of Israel, uncovering your nakedness in front of your servants, like only a foolish would."

"I didn't uncover in front of anyone but my God, and yes, I will make myself worthless to Him. As for my servants, they are the ones that will honor me."

She remained embittered in her detestation and scorn, and departed to be but a past; a past that had secretly loved him for his greatness and boldness, a past that had longed for him and protected him, when the king wanted to kill him. A past that wouldn't find peace in his glory as king and wouldn't approve with the loss of her father's life, who was the one that had taught her to be proud and pompous, who was the only king she ever knew. She left like a distant pain, like a past that gave him his manhood, but gave her poison and loss for all that her life was before he entered into it, as a crowned king. As he was thinking on the love that she had given him, the hate and the scorn, the barrenness of her spirit, he realized that he was still walking on the terrace, and somewhere in the tail of his eye he captured something that was moving.

***

Curiosity took his sight to a slightly opened window, where he could notice in that half-darkened night the pleasing body of a graceful woman, whose face was reflecting sweetness in that embrace of night with the glowing splendor of the moon. He felt like his eyelashes were touching every dewdrop of water that had moistened her body, and the smoothness and softness of her milky skin filled his flesh with a rushing force of blood. Her brown hair, kissed by the sparkles of the stars, the eyes that gave charm to the night, her lips like sweet wine, her cheeks like fresh fruit, her delicate neck like a swan, her unadulterated shoulders, and her upright breasts, her belly like a field of drizzled green grass, her waist like a graceful stream, her legs like two marbled pillars, engraved with skillfulness; made him realize that none of his women was as perfect as she was, was as desirable as she was. He was stunned and lost in front of all he saw, and felt being in the middle of a struggle where he desired to fail.

***

A refreshing evening breeze helped him restrain these emotions, even though inside, he still was disturbed. He moved his feet that weren't obeying, and with his mind possessed by this woman, walked toward his room. He was surprised at himself. He had never desired a woman this way before and never had he thought of her beauty so deeply. He was trying to convince himself that his wives were as beautiful as she, but her image stood like a soft-lighted shadow in his soul. "Was she married? To whom was she married?" These two questions made him feel exhausted and scared that she really was married to someone. He felt shame for this yearning that had invaded his heart and felt sadness at the thought that she might never be his. He looked around and found himself in his bed. Never had that bed been so big and so empty, nor had his room been filled so much with dreams and thoughts like that night. Scared that God would catch sight of this startling desire, he tried to gather one by one, all he had put into his mind, and bury them in the deep sea of his heart. He felt love for that woman, he felt need for her, and he felt embarrassed for all his feelings, because she could belong to someone else. He felt shame before his God, and for the first time he didn't talk to Him for this beautiful thing that he experienced, he felt shame, because this time his heart was beating in injustice. He didn't speak a word; he didn't even ask for forgiveness. Touched with yearning, he felt chills go through his body, and his eyes shed tears of sorrow. Darkness was torturing him with thoughts and feelings he had never known before, and he felt mortified from all of them.

He got off his bed hoping he would get away from all that emptiness, and noticed that the sunrise was shedding light all around. It had kissed the earth with its dew, and had given everything sweetness, which he wanted to embrace with his spirit and rest there, forgetting all that had happened. But the only way he could rest that morning would be finding a way and a reason to ask for that woman, without anyone understanding his intentions. That moment his servant knocked lightly on the door. He turned his head toward the door and allowed him to enter.

"My lord, your servant has brought you the basin with water for your morning cleansing."

"Come here, near my window," he ordered, trying to keep the normality of his voice that was shaking from restlessness and fatigue. His servant approached humbly and made all the preparations ready for his cleansing.

"My lord is a little anxious, I see," he spoke with a depleted voice, but the king, trying to show him kindness, replied:

"No, I was just looking at the building in front. All my officers are in the battlefield and they have left their families here. I heard the voice of a child and I was moved. Really, do you know who of my officers lives there?" And he pointed at the window where he had seen that enchanting woman the night before.

"My lord," answered the servant," Uriah the Hittite lives there, he is married to Bath-Sheba, daughter of Eliam, but they have no children. They have been married for about two years, and now, he is in war.

That name gave a new reflection to the image he had in mind, and not only that, but also a chance for him to call it.

"My lord, would you allow me to leave?" Asked the servant as he was gathering the things he had brought with him in the room.

"Yes," answered the king, "also, I don't want breakfast served today."

He moved away from the window and walked toward the door. His steps took him to the waiting room where the courier had just arrived with news from the battlefield. He was walking and thinking about the news he was about to receive and for the first time was forgetting about the image of the night that had disturbed his sleep and his dreams. He remembered that never before a courier had to bring him news from war, because he had always been there. May be God had let him stay in the palace so that he would fight the biggest fight of his life there? Was the night that had just passed only the beginning of a war tougher than any other before? He was realizing that the enemy was not the tribes around Israel, but the king of Israel, he was his own enemy. For the first time in life he was afraid of war.

***

He lifted up his eyes that were looking down as if they were searching for his bravery, and saw he was in the room, and the courier was waiting for him to sit so that he could give him the news. He greeted the courier and sat to listen to him, but his ears were not attentive to anything but to what was boiling in his heart and mind. He was overwhelmed with fear and agony; he was trying to concentrate on the news of a war where he knew how to win, but no news, no effort was withdrawing him from that turmoil that had started within him. Everything seemed empty and meaningless, and the torturing image of the night became once again his news, his desire, his hate, his war.

The courier had stopped and was waiting for the king to give him orders for the commander of the army, Joab, but David was silent and lost in another war, which he was trying to hide from the curious eyes of the counselors who were with him in the room. He noticed one of them stand up and speak:

"Forgive me, my king, for being forward and speaking, but I think Joab should stay longer in these positions and learn more about the surroundings and the army of these people."

The courier was still waiting for him to give instructions, but all the king gave was a movement of his head approving the words of his counselor, and finally said:

"You may depart."

As the door closed, he approached one of his underlings and asked him to bring Bath-Sheba. Even though surprised at the king's request, he swallowed his curiosity, and without making any questions he left toward her residence. After a while he was back standing in front of the king with her. With a control that gave no doubts he ordered his servants to leave the room, and when they were alone, he got closer to that creature that had seized his mind, heart and body.

"Here I am my lord, your servant," she spoke with a voice that sounded like twitter filling the room.

He softly took off the cover she had on her head, and touched her smooth and shining brown hair, her face, her body... he was feeling her inside himself.

Bath-Sheba went home with memories in her mind and soul, with memories that flowed like tears from her watery eyes. Fear, sadness and joy filled her entire being. "Oh, what if something happens…I am married, I belong to my husband alone… My king desires me!"

Her nanny walking behind her, fastened her steps and got in front to open the door, and she realized they had arrived home. Everything reminded her of her husband, but things now had changed. She felt compassion and obedience rather than love and commitment; sadly closed her eyes, and everything she found inside herself was he, the king and his yearning. She dried up the tears that clouded her vision and noticed that, Azubah, her nanny, was there, filled with impatience to hear her sorrow. Bath-Sheba knew well her faithfulness and her wisdom; she knew that she alone could understand the experiences of her soul. She got near her, took a hold of her hands to feel her warmth, and looked deeply into her attentive eyes and spoke in distress:

"Last night, as you were helping me bathe, I felt something more than warm water go over my body. Something got my attention, and I sighted with the tail of my eye someone on the terrace of the palace. I felt shame for my nakedness, but I didn't want to give the impression that I had seen that someone, even though I was curious to know who that person was. Standing motionless, although I couldn't see his eyes, I could feel their sight touch me all over. Then I saw his shadow move slowly toward the king's room, and in that moment I felt that something would soon change my life. I was so frightened that I banished all I had sensed by bringing near me Uriah and his love. When I lay down to sleep, I had a strange battle inside me, but still, after a while I was able to sleep. When I woke up in the morning, I realized I had spent one of the most beautiful nights of my life. Dreams full of colors and rainbows had been my night's guests. Oh, Azubah, I was so happy when I woke up!"

She stopped for one moment to breathe and to dry up the tears that had started to loosen the knot in her chest. Azubah took her sweet face in her hands, touched her softly and wrapped her in her motherly embrace. After she calmed down a little bit, she started speaking again:

"When you came and told me that the king had asked for me in the palace, I understood that what I had felt was part of his frozen eyesight upon me, and I understood that something was about to change. As I was preparing myself to go before him, I felt control and haste in my actions. As I was walking I could see myself hesitate and hurry and when I got there, I saw the king waiting for me to belong to him, and I obeyed to the desire of a man that I was desiring too; I obeyed, forgetting that I would have to come back to my past! Now, I really don't know what is going to happen! I tremble when I think that I might have gotten pregnant… What about my husband, will I love him like I did before? And… will I see the king, my lord, again?"

She broke out in tears that wouldn't find peace anywhere, but in an uncertain future. Azubah embraced her as if she would take away from her soul all pain and doubt, and with inaudible words she spoke to her eyes that were thirsty for solace: "Everything will be okay!" In silence she spoke her wisdom, she talked to her soul that was crushed down with her world with a wordless commitment, but that had more voice than the young woman's sobs; with hands that tousled her hair she said: "My daughter, don't try to find answers to questions that you shouldn't have asked! Perhaps you did have the choice of disobeying to those feelings you experienced, but everything has a reason, and the future will show us the sin or the justice, the curse or the blessing. Don't shed tears, but give patience to your heart…"

***

Bath-Sheba was confined in her nanny's chest and was staying there to hear every voiceless thought, feel every touch of goodness, every tear of love. Azubah had been the mirror where she had shown every detail of her life. She had seen her grow up, become a girl, a woman… and now she felt she was more than a woman, she was a sad being for she had lived happiness. She looked up, and with a voice that hesitated to hear itself, asked:

"Beloved Azubah, do you remember when I met with Uriah for the first time? Do you remember what I told you?"

For the first time Azubah laughed. That smile brought glimmer on Bath-Sheba's face.

"My daughter, you didn't speak, you sang. You sang me a song that still makes me laugh, it's like I hear you now singing it." She caressed her face and started singing:

"A *lonely star was left in the sky*
Without a gleam
Without a beam
And tired as it was it fell from stream
To come and rest in your singing dream!"

Bath-Sheba laughed as she was whispering the words, and when Azubah finished singing, she hugged her as if she was hugging that song that had remained untouched in the safety of the past. She learned that song from Uriah himself, when she first met him at the courtyard in front of her house. That day they played hide and seek, but he always found her; he enfolded her with his infancy, and then sang to her that song with which he was raised. He was taller than her, dark skin and black hair, big hazel eyes with a deep color where everything was pure and sweet. He would take her by the hand, and together they would run following one another, they would laugh and play, and there was nothing that would spoil the innocence and sweetness of their childhood days. Those times taught them the colors of the fields and mountains, taught them the azure of the sky, as they laid to see the shapes of the clouds that flew in the limitless space; taught them the stars, that were the promise of their people, taught them that they were the purity, the dream, the peace of each-other. They loved one another when they didn't know how to kiss, when holding hands was more than an embrace, when "good night" was the night's first dream, when "good morning" was the first ray of sun. Her hair was like breath of life to him, and his hand was the refuge she always needed to feel. Their eyes were gazes filled with infinity, and life was the meaning they found in each other. That meaning became commitment and love, when their childhood departed like spring to leave place to summer become their season, their marriage.

***

But their song didn't change, nor did their embrace, their kiss, their gaze. And as she was rejoicing in the love of the past, she found herself again in the uncertainty of the present. How could everything have changed from a look in the dark? How could love become unknown to her, when she had lived it with Uriah? How could doubt that she now had for life, become so desirable? She got up from Azubah's lap and went by the window with hope that the future would greet her there with the same certainty that past had said good-bye. She lifted her eyes up to the heavens, but all she saw, was the king's palace, was the terrace where he had given her his first look, his first love. She passed her hand on her chest to feel his last embrace, then on her stomach to feel once again that lived love, and with a tremble in her voice, she whispered: "I love you, even though I don't know you, I love you, even though I don't know what you'll give to me, I love you, even though you're in darkness, I love you, I love you, because I can't otherwise!"

Hushed, she entered in Azubah's chest again. Poured herself in her embrace and stayed in the solitude of that darkness, that awoke from the voice of her nanny.

"My daughter, God's ways are mysterious, not like our ways, where we know everything, where nothing is unexpected. Remember Sarah, she gave birth when her womb was dry from the old age; think of Miriam, Moses' sister, she became a prophet of God when slavery had overcome Israel; think of Rahab, she was but a prostitute, but she was saved from the Lord and she helped our people in the battle of Jericho…"

"Azubah!" She stopped her, "these are women who lived God's promise, He chose them. How am I chosen here? What did I do, Azubah? Am I the reason to the king's sin, why did I let something like this happen, why? He is chosen by the Lord's heart, Azubah, he should remain king to His glory, not to His shame. I made him break the Law, that Law that he loves with all his might. Remember how he danced when he brought the Ark of the Covenant in the city? Did I make him forget the promise he has given to the Lord?"

Azubah took Bath-Sheba's face in her compassionate hands, looked her in the eyes and spoke:

"All those women were unprepared for the mission they were given, none of them knew what God had in store for them…" she stopped as if she didn't want to speak for something that had to be kept hidden, and after a while continued:

"Don't torture yourself this way, let tomorrow worry for its own troubles, hope in goodness and grace, not punishment of a mistake. May be your mistake was not what you gave to the king, but your life till now."

"Azubah, what are you saying? How can what happened be good, there is no way it doesn't deserve the punishment of the Law."

"We are human and we don't always recognize our mistakes. Our mind is too small to understand God's plans, He's the one who created the world from nothing, He turns what's wrong into right, and emptiness into abundance. What I am saying is that you don't judge yourself, or the king. Let what happened become part of the future, if God allows it."

They remained in silence with the hope that future would calmly come without judgment or punishment; with the hope that the sun would shine for the good and the bad, the rain would fall for the righteous and the unrighteous, and God would pour down His grace for the holy and the sinners.

***

A few weeks had passed by, and her life once again, had become a safe past, where Uriah was her love and commitment, where childhood was her song, where the king was, but a denied love that was dreaming in the past.

She woke up, like every morning, with a smile on her lips and with a song in her heart, but something like a butterfly went through her tummy and made her dizzy. She felt tired, her body was fatigued, there was a yellow like shadow on her face and she felt like she was going to take out all she had in her empty stomach. Azubah went near her and helped her lie down again.

"My daughter, what happened? I have told you many times not to get off your bed quickly."

"Azubah, I don't feel well. I've had this tight feeling on my breasts these past few days, and finally now it has gone, but has taken away all my strength and has left me with a heavy stomach. I'm nauseous and everything inside me is in commotion."

Azubah's face changed color as if she too, was feeling Bath-Sheba's malady, and with a frightened voice she asked her:

"My daughter, you are expecting the king's child and you haven't told me?"

"Azubah, how can I say anything, how can I not silence this news, this is the fear and the desire of a dream, this is not the truth I want to live. I love this child, I love him with an eternal happiness, I love him with a love I've never experienced before, I love him with a fear that torments me because I desire for this child to live for me and I want to live for him. When I first thought I was pregnant my heart broke in two: I had this immeasurable joy, and also a terrible fear; every moment that passed by, filled my being with thrills for the new life inside me, and with cries that this life weren't true, but just a mistake of my body. With my heart I longed to feel this life inside me, and at the same time, I would cast away all desires of having this child and I wished that everything would be forgotten where it was conceived, there, in darkness. Oh, how I want that you tell me that there is no life in my womb that everything is but a sickness that will go away, o, how I want it to be a sickness that will heal me from my fears that will separate me from the past, from that dream, from the king. O, how I wish that all this is but a dream that will end when I open my eyes, and awake to find myself again a wife to my husband, to my Uriah. Azubah, I remember how Uriah and I would talk about our first child. I remember him touching my face softly with his hands and speaking to me so sweetly: 'You will be the only mother of my children!' and I would say to him: 'And you will be the only father to my children!'... These dreams are gone; I have betrayed his faith and his love."

Now her commotion had turned into weeping and pain that didn't find healing anywhere.

Azubah stood silent. Then she took a comb and started combing her hair, like she would do every morning. She breathed deeply and started to speak:

"You know my life, you know my losses and what I want to say now is that you don't wish loss upon your life. Don't ask of this child that he not be, don't lament his coming. Don't let this joy that you feel as a mother, be killed by doubt and fear, and don't let the life inside you live with the bitterness of your uncertainty... When I first learned that I was going to be a mother, I lived the greatest joy and happiness of my life, but that was stolen by pain and loss. God didn't allow that I become a mother, and I lost my child before I could give him birth. O, my daughter, how I wish that you never have to go through such agony."

"What about the king? Do I have to tell him? What will he say?" Bath-Sheba interrupted.

"I will give the king the news of your pregnancy, my daughter."

***

These words made Bath-Sheba unvoiced again. She felt darkness invading her heart and bringing back the doubts that she had tried to keep away from herself ever since she had left the palace. Now fear and anguish of the king's acceptance would be her new dwelling, her cry for help would be life itself.

-3-

He was sad. The joy that moments ago had filled his soul, now had thrown him into a pit of despair, a despair that was blaming him for that blind love, that love that he gave to his selfishness. In his fingers he was still holding her smile; on his body he was wearing her gleaming skin, and with his ears he could still hear the sound of her singing voice. Memories made him a stranger to himself, who he couldn't stop accusing for all that had happened. Azubah's image was standing in front of him with that rebuking attitude saying: "My lord, your servant, my lady Bath-Sheba has sent me to tell you that she's expecting a child."

***

The joy that a part of him would always be with her, quenched immediately when he thought of the Law and the rights it gave to her husband. Like an echo screaming from the hidden caves of his soul, he heard the unshakable words of the Law: "If a man is found in bed with a married woman, they both shall be killed…"

With the passion of a moment he had punished himself and the woman that he loved. How could he hide his guilt? He knew that God was his refuge, his secret place, but not now. Now he had become shameful to himself with something so beautiful. How could God accept him, when he didn't accept himself? No, now he was on his own, and he had to think of something so that he or his beloved, or the child would not be punished.

Speechless, perplexed, stuck in his soul's deception, he recalled God's faithfulness, his own faithfulness toward God, he thought of that covenant that had made him special and different from Saul, the covenant of love and trust he had with God.

***

He had been king not for too long, when all the leaders of the tribes came to him with gifts and gratitude accepting him as king of all Israel and built him a palace in the city that he named after himself: City of David. Masterminded carpenters and bricklayers came and poured out their skills in building that palace, where he put his family, lived God's faithfulness, and became king. Many times he had walked through the corridors of that palace, many times he had meditated on the terrace, and many times he had heard the cries and the laughters of the children filling the air. How many times had he heard the tip toeing steps of his concubines that walked with their heads down like buds that would bloom at the sound of his voice. How many times, the leaders of his army had shaken the foundations of that palace, in their rush to bring news from the battlefield. How many experiences, how many promises this palace held inside. And now, now he was filling it with the image of the one who had invaded his everything, even his faithfulness. He would dream of her walking that would make the tiles sound with joy, he would dream of the air moving through her clothes, the space fill with her voice, the house satisfy with the creature she would bring.

But how would he make her his own? How would he bring to light what was betrayal and death for them both?

***

Meanwhile the courier had just arrived with the latest news from the battle. The king walked toward the salon with the same fight like a few weeks ago; a fight with himself, a fight to win an injustice, a fight where love was the enemy. His white robe, reminded him of the times when he was proud of wearing it, but now it seemed dirty from what he had done, he felt unworthy for that robe, unworthy of sitting on the king's throne. But he had to sit so that the courier would start with the news. Approaching the throne, a thought that came so unexpectedly, made him sit.

As the courier finished giving the news, he stood waiting for orders from the king, who wasn't silent like before. With an almost uncontrolled attitude the king spoke:

"Tell Joab to stay in the positions he has taken. For the time being I want him to send to me Uriah with his men, so that they can tell me in a detailed report what they have seen, and how they think we should make our offensive. I want them to show me where they have seen the weak positions of our enemy and where we should concentrate our forces.

I understand this will delay us," he continued, so that he could justify himself against the unasked questions that his counselors were about to rise, "but we should be confident of our victory."

"Yes" said the courier; "Is there anything else my lord?"

David looked around for his counselors' approval and said:

"No, you may depart."

He stood on the throne holding an icy hope for help inside his soul. A feeling of anxiety was making him leave the room, but he had to stay.

***

Like every morning he asked his servant to allow the people who were waiting outside to get in. They had come with their problems and troubles so that he would hear them and help them. He would become part of their lives giving them his advice or interfering with his power giving them the justice they needed. They all loved him, because he was their shepherd, he was the chosen one; he was their leader, their victor. As he was standing there, with his head on his left hand, he noticed a woman with tearful eyes holding a child by the hand. The child looked happy in his mother's arms, who couldn't hide the worry and was waiting humbly to come before the king.

He signaled the servant to bring her before him. The woman moved toward with a fast but calm step. She tried to dry out the tears of hope and sadness that had made her eyes red and waited for the king to hear her story.

"My daughter, tell me what has brought you here today!"

"My lord, my king," she started to speak trying to contain her sobbing, "I want to thank you for this honor that you give me by letting me speak before you. This child, who seems so happy, is so, because he still doesn't know. His mother, my sister, she was expecting her second child, but she passed away from a very severe sickness. His father is in the battlefield, fighting for the king, my lord, and he doesn't know anything. He left with the joy of life, but now I have to give him the news of its loss and the loss of the woman that would bring that life. She stopped to hold the child that started running in the salon.

For a moment the king didn't speak. He wasn't impatient to leave the room anymore, but something like a strong knife was holding his throat like never before. Many times he had had to send bad news to his soldiers, but this news was different. The words of that woman made him think more deeply of Bath-Sheba. The fear that she too, might lose her life or the child from a sickness during the pregnancy made his knees shake and his body fill with chills, but his mind took him far, where his fighters were. Who was that father, that man, that soldier, to whom he would have to give this bitter news? How would he speak so that his pain would not be too heavy on his heart?

He stood up and said:

"My daughter, I have no words to comfort you, because there is no comfort for death. I will send the news of this loss and I will have the father of this child come back home. Let him find comfort in his son. Give my official the father's name. May God grant you his peace. You may go."

**

He sat again with pain in his heart and saw as that woman was leaving with joy and sadness. Other people came before him and he spoke to them, and helped them. But his heart was poisoned as he constantly thought of that strange woman, that hadn't been able to give birth to life and rejoice her offspring. He was terrified at the thought that this could happen to Bath-Sheba. He remembered again that he had to free her from the Law; he had to cleanse her from the betrayal. With the hope that everything would go well, and that no one would know about their infidelity, his mind was pierced again by the dreadful thought that had come to him before he listened to the unfortunate news of that woman. When the waiting time was over, he got off his throne and went to his room with the fear and the responsibility that he had to set Bath-Sheba free from any kind of loss or punishment. Now he had to wait for Uriah to come; he would be his salvation, he would be Bath-Sheba's deliverance.

He entered into his room and understood that all he had to do is wait patiently and evenly, but how could he wait and have peace, when the thought that, things could get worse grew stronger? He tried to encourage himself and the stressed hours with the idea that in the end something good would come out of all this mess of feelings and actions.

**

It was the first time that he was doing something alone, without asking for God's help. He felt culpable and he couldn't face Him. It was the first time he was forgetting that man can't be redeemed by his own righteousness. This can only be done with God's mercy.

For now he had a thought and he was trying to find every little detail to make it a plan that would save him, Bath-Sheba, and the child. He would do anything to give her the chance to live life and enjoy the new being that was blooming in her womb. He would do anything to feel again the joy of being a father, like he had felt it when his other women had given him children. But now this joy was different and full of life, because Bath-Sheba wasn't just a woman, she was a promise made in darkness, a desire lived in passion, a love that would give him more than a child; it would give him an heir to the throne.

With these thoughts in his mind he was walking and found himself on the terrace again. Bath-Sheba's window was closed, but now he didn't need that window to think of her. He gave that woman adultery and love, he gave her himself and his ego, he gave her life and death, and he gave her a child. And now she needed more than just protection from the Law, more than hiding of the truth, she needed her life to become a future without fear, a future where he would be more than a king; he would be the lord of her love.

He slowly walked away from the terrace toward his room, where the night would be long again, it would be a friend that would bring him thoughts and solutions; it would be war where he would have to win.

4

U riah and his men were entering the city. They had been traveling for days, but for Uriah this journey had seemed shorter than his life. The war had changed him, but it hadn't made him forget his beloved, his dearest Bath-Sheba not even for one moment. Her face had followed him everywhere, in the footpaths of this war, in the restless nights, in his talks with the other men, in the morning's dew that wet his sleepless eyes; in everything that had kept him awake in that unending war. The men behind him they laughed with his passion and teased him with their words: "Now we won't hear of Bath-Sheba for a while, you think we'll see anything, though?" They laughed, but Uriah spoke with a voice that tried to hide its sadness:

"I will not be able to enter into my home. Don't you understand that this return is not for me? We're returning for the king. My heart would laugh with you, but right now the king has called me, and I have to respond to his call."

***

They didn't talk anymore as if they felt the same sadness as he and, as they were entering the city they felt its peace be fiercer than the war where they were coming from. The streets were quiet. Here and there they heard the noise of someone washing dishes in the courtyard, the laughter of some child playing, or greetings from those few people in the street that saw them proudly and rejoiced in their bravery.

"Hello warriors, how are you?"

They greeted back with the movement of their head as if saying: "We're there for you!"

"We wish you bring good news, and we wish you victory!" Shouted a woman as she was holding a pot of water and stopped them to quench their thirst. But the king's waiting was stronger than their thirst, and thanking her they continued their way to the palace.

A child cried out with joy as he saw his father: "Daddy is here!"

His mother ran outside with a laughter that brought tears of longing in her eyes. She took the child in her arms, and with the crowd, followed after them as they were going toward the palace.

Uriah could not withhold the shiver that was going through his body, and could not hide the look that was searching for Bath-Sheba in the crowd. The people now were crying out loud, some of joy, some of longing, some of sadness of a war that had become inevitable.

***

They were promised this land of honey and milk, but they had to fight to make it their own. Some of the women looked at the soldiers and cried to comfort the loss they felt inside. Children ran after them with promises that they too would become fighters when they grew up. In the midst of all that commotion of movements and cries, Uriah distinguished the tearful eyes of Azubah, and beside her Bath-Sheba with her head down. Under the head kerchief he could see her hair trying to dance their way out in the breeze, in the hands that were covering her glowing face, he could see some tears waiting to dry, and on her shoulders he saw a shaking that pierced his heart. He waved his hand with the hope that it would soften a little the wanting nostalgia, and standing on his horse he thought of this war that was keeping them apart.

This war was the first separation they had lived, the first longing, and the first fight with loneliness, partition, and distance. Duty for the people was something that he took pride on, but this pride couldn't smother the love he had for Bath-Sheba. He had loved her ever since he was a child with an eternal love, sincere and true. He was little when he had seen her drawing on the ground in front of her house, and he had gone near to admire the sun she had created. He remembered how she hid herself behind a fallen wall, near her house, and when he found her, he hugged her as if saying that he would always keep her there, in his embrace, even when he grew up. He remembered how she cried with him, when he lost his mother, he remembered how she held his hand on the day his brother got married, and he remembered when he saw pictured in her eyes that childhood sun, when they became one.

***

These memories were racing in his mind, when he and the others found themselves in front of the king's palace gates. Everything seemed withered from the heat. The azure sky was moaning from an unseen anxiety, and the sun was burning as if committing a cruel mission that the fate had assigned it to accomplish. He stopped to inform the guards of their arrival in the palace, and without getting off the horse, turned his head one more time to see Bath-Sheba's and Azubah's shadows leaving. In his heart he had a blazing desire to meet with the love of his life, but there were no flames that would make him forget the most important obligation he had: the meeting with the king.

**

Once the guard allowed them to enter, they got in, leaving behind the gates that were closing. The king had ordered that an area of the courtyard be prepared for their stay. The tents had been set up, there were tables in an open area, and on the other side of the plaza there were basins for their cleansing. They got off their horses, and for the first time they felt the fatigue walking with their feet. The journey had really been long, but war and nostalgia had made it feel short. Their voices started to fill the emptiness of the plaza that looked panting from that suffocating heat. As they were refreshing themselves with water that the servants were bringing from the palace, one of the guards came to Uriah to make known to him the time they should appear before the king. At that moment, scenes of fighting become so alive; he felt he had never left the battlefield. In his mind came moments that reminded him when he had been hiding in the enemy's camp, when he was trying to learn their guards schedule, when he was running to bring the news on time, when the fighting was more than fighting, it was survival.

**

The dusk was falling in the city and the noises were dying. The voice of the cicadas was spoiling the tranquility of the night, and it was lullabying the people to sleep. Uriah was looking at his men, who were all laying down to rest, and he too, was trying to find some comfort in this peaceful night. But something in his heart was keeping him awake. His spirit was restless and his mind was murmuring with strange thoughts. Though far from the war, he was thinking how close his life was to it. Though he wasn't scared of death, something was making him believe that it was near. He thought of Bath-Sheba, their love, how her heart would heal if he were not to be. He was struggling under the covers and couldn't find any rest. He got up and started walking in the courtyard. He lifted up his head to see the sky, that endless space of stars and darkness, just like his heart, filled with love, and now for the first time with doubt.

***

It felt as if his steps were awakening the day and the dawn was greeting with its first rays of the sun. He looked inside his heart to see if the same dawn was rising there, pushing away the doubt of the night, but all he found was the vastness of a starry darkness. He started to get back to the tents and saw that his friends were waiting for him. He walked to the other side of the plaza, where the basins were, and after he cleansed himself, he sat in one of the tables that had been prepared for them to have breakfast. Even though he wasn't hungry, he ate, and that made him ready to go before the king. And again this thought tightened his soul, and worsened the doubt he had felt during the night. As he was trying to get away from it, one of his friends patted him on the shoulder and said:

"Uriah, the guard is here to take us to the king. We're all ready."

They left, and the guard was with them. The palace was glorious, built with stones that were brought from far away, with chandeliers put on pillars to illuminate the nights, layered with tiles with a six angular star sculptured on, to remind them that God had in control every part of the universe. As they were walking through the corridors they come across different aspects of the king's life, and they were all amazed at its abundance; his women, his children, his officials, workers, guards, everything in its place and order. They found themselves in the main salon, where David was waiting sited on the throne. He got up and with an extension of his hand he invited them to stand before him.

"Uriah, men, I want to thank you for this journey you had to take, according to my request." he started to speak. "Meanwhile, Uriah, I want you to inform me in details about your observations, and openly share with me your viewpoint about this war."

He stood before the king and for one moment it seemed like he was watching the anointing that prophet Samuel had performed on him a long time ago. He could see the illumination of that holy anointing on the king's hair, in his eyes he could see a hidden passion for God, and all around in that salon, in that palace, the blessing of the Lord upon his life. All this made him think: "Is the king satisfied with all he has?" He was surprised at this question he asked himself, and knowing he wouldn't get

30

any answer from anyone, moved forward from where he was standing, greeted the king, and started to speak.

"My king, my lord, I am so honored from your request, and the place I have in this magnificent army. I surely can say that the battle belongs to us, we know the enemy's protection points, their guards schedule, we know all about the life in that place, when they sleep and when they rise, we know the number of their soldiers, their weaponry, we also know that the Lord is with us and will give us the victory. Their strongest position is at the city's gates, but we've been prepared to put there our best and bravest; and with God's blessing this land and this war will belong to us."

As he was speaking, he noticed the interest that the king was showing about all he was saying, and he felt proud in his approval. After he said all he had to say, he stepped back to his friends, and waited for the king to speak. But to everyone's surprise, all the king said was this:

"I know your bravery, your fight; I know the commitment you have toward our people. I also know that you've been away from your families, your wives, and children; away from the ones who love you and are your support here. It is a small gift of gratitude that I want to offer you for your service and loyalty toward the king, and the people, that I allow you to spend this night into your homes.

He felt the king's hand on his shoulders, and then leave, but he remained motionless and stunned from those words.

5

The king had seen Uriah's arrival from the terrace of the palace. The people had followed them with cheers of longing and joy, and he remembered how he had been followed once, with cheers of praise and glory. He remembered when he chose Uriah to be one of his soldiers, also remembered the promise he had given to himself to be the shepherd of this army, and the protector of its soldiers. But now, he was standing there, knowing that he had to deceive one of them. But the thought that in this deception would find salvation everyone that his love and unfaithfulness had put to risk, made him believe that what he had in mind was right and the only way out.

He felt someone pulling the robe he had on his shoulders. Turned back his head and saw one of his daughters that was laughing and asking for his attention.

"Father," she said "I see that soldiers have come from the battlefield, I want to meet them. I want to see how you looked like when you fought. I also have made embroidery of a beautiful medallion with your star father; I want to give it to Uriah. I saw how he got off the horse and I think he is the bravest of all!"

He put his hand through her black curls, embraced her, kissed her on the cheeks and saw deep into her gentle eyes. She was Tamara, the girl that loved everything. To her everything was pure and without mistakes, she had a beautiful and endless spirit, and desired to learn and know everything. He had given her a lamb, when she was little, and it seemed as if they both were the same creature, hungry for pastures, thirsty for valleys with fresh water, ravenous for eternity. As he was looking into her eyes that were shining of love and joy that she felt when she was near him, she spoke again:

"Father, I have made a song. Will you play the harp with me, please? Here, I brought it for you."

He smiled and nodded. He sat on a stone, took the harp from her hand, and for some reason it felt heavy. It had been some time since he had sung and he felt guilt inside his accusing soul. But it wasn't time to listen to the accusations of his soul; his little Tamara was waiting impatiently to sing her first song.

"I will sing to you o Lord with all my heart.
I will tell of all your wanders!
I will rejoice in you and I will be pleased in you.
I will glorify your name o, Most High!
You that guard my lamb from the wolves when he grazes in the fields
You that love me and have given me endless spaces
You have given me the best father in the world
And have made him the greatest king of times.
La la la la la la la la la la la la la la la la la la la la la."

She sang with her eyes closed as if she was looking God inside, and tapped her foot on the tiles of the terrace. It felt as if that tapping made the entire palace cheer with her song. She played with her little hands the harp, that her father, David himself, had made, and with her lips she chanted the sweetest sounds; the sounds of a voice that seemed like flying all the way up to the sky and danced with the white clouds, releasing dew drops on earth and refreshing everything and everyone that desired to worship God. He hugged her and remembered that he had taught her how to play, how to take care of her little lamb; it was he that had rooted the love for the Creator in her heart, it was he, he, to whom now, everything clean and wonderful seemed far and strange. But she spoke without letting go of his embrace:

"Father, you're not singing. Please sing to me one of your songs. You know which song I like best." She jumped from his lap, and with a playful joy she said: "No, you have to guess, guess which one of the songs you have taught me, is the one I like best."

He could see her joy and with his mind he tried to solve her riddle. He looked away at the courtyard, as if he would find his answer there, and saw that the men, who had just arrived, were washing up. Deep inside he wanted to do the same, and without thinking, he started singing to his little girl that was keenly waiting to hear his voice in song:

"O my Lord, don't correct me in your anger
And don't punish me in the fire of your wrath.
Have mercy on me o, Lord.
For evil is torturing me.

Heal me o Lord, for my bones are suffering.
Mm mm mm mm mm mm mm mm mm mm."

She was startled and looked at him saying:

"Father, what have you done that you feel so bad? Haven't you taught me that the Lord loves you, that you do everything after God's heart, why do you think He is going to punish you? Why are you sad? Have you forgotten to speak with the Lord, why, why?"

Her endless questioning and her sadness made him heartbroken. He didn't know how to comfort her and how to hide himself from her. She had been like a mirror where he had reflected everything beautiful and good, but now, now he had to hide and conceal himself from her.

"My daughter, I sang that song because I thought you would like it. Remember how you forgot to feed your lamb one time, and he got sick? Remember how you despaired, and prayed to God to save him? I am sorry my darling, I didn't mean to upset you. Now I'll think better, and I'll come in your room tonight, before you go to sleep, and I'll sing to you your favorite song. Now go, it's getting late. I'll come to see you later."

"Father, what about the medallion I embroidered, when can I give it to Uriah?"

"They will be here for a few days, my daughter. We have time."

He kissed her and saw her run with the harp in her hand and with a song in her mouth. But in his heart, the song he had just sung was bursting with powerful tones. He lifted up his head toward the sky that was becoming dark from the dusk and said: "I am sorry I lied to my daughter; I couldn't tell her the truth. Oh, it is the first time I lied to her, how did I do that?"

And as he was looking at the sky, its endless space, he remembered he hadn't confessed to the Lord his pain, his ordeal, his passion, his sin. He put his head down and whispered: "Not even you I can tell. You can't understand me, because I have sinned; you can't accept me, because not even I can live with myself right now. When will all this be over? Ah, Bath-Sheba, Bath-Sheba, I wish you are well and may everything turn out well, too!" He looked at the courtyard again, and saw that the men were now resting. He was motionless and realized that he was standing at the same place where he had stood the first time he saw Bath-Sheba. His body shivered as if he was seeing her again, and as he was thinking of her, he saw someone coming out of the tent, and walk as if trying to find something lost. His steps were heavy from something invisible that was not fatigue, but doubt, as if what he had lost was there, somewhere near, in that very courtyard. He looked closely and noticed that it was Uriah. The night he first saw Bath-Sheba flashed in his mind like it was written in the darkness and was waiting for the light. The cicadas were singing, the stars were shining; everything seemed like speaking of that unforgettable, eternal, night that he had to bury into his heart.

***

He recalled, he had promised Tamara to sing her, her favorite song, and rushed in the palace, toward his daughter's room, where the little torch-holder was still burning over her head bed that was adorned with different kind of embroideries that she had made.

"Father, " she whispered with a sleepy voice, " I thought you'd forget. Did you guess which song I like?" And a smile twinkled on her face.

He sat on the side of her bed, folded her little hand with his, and started to sing a song that was shuddering in his voice.

"O Lord, our Lord, how majestic is your name
In all the earth!
You have set your glory above the heavens!
Out of the mouth of babes and sucklings you have ordained glory!"

She threw herself into his arms, kissed him on the cheek, where a tear was falling to get lost, there, in her pure kiss.

"Father, you didn't forget, father!"

"No, my daughter," he spoke softly, "now go to sleep, it is very late. What will you say to me now, where do you keep God?"

"Here, where eternity is, daddy, in my heart." She said, and put her hand on her heart. "What about you daddy, where do you keep God? Aren't you going to tell me tonight?"

He quickly put his hand on his chest, and slid it down, so that he wouldn't feel the emptiness there, and without saying another word, he got off the bed. He bended down to give her one good night kiss on her forehead, and as he was leaving he blew off the flame from the torch.

***

He felt lonelier than ever. In a very meaningless way he had drifted away from God, his daughter, and himself. He didn't blame himself for loving Bath-Sheba, but for having to save that love

6

She ran in the dusty streets when she heard of him coming, with the hope that he would be her forgiveness, her redemption. Azubah followed her with the head kerchief in her hand, which she forgot to put on from the rush, and with those soft old hands of hers, tried to hold her and throw it on her head.

"My daughter, I am as fervent to go as you are, I want to be there now, but you can't go out without covering your head."

"O, Azubah, it feels like I never have the head kerchief off, as if I'm always covered. But I don't want to be covered any more, I want to be free, do you know what I mean? But I know you're right; I can't go out without it. What about my clothes; is my tummy visible?"

"No my dear, everything is still hidden, don't worry about it for now."

Her eyes were full of tears, and her heart was beating fast from fear and joy. Her feet stumbled in the dust as she was trying to make them run toward the main street, where Uriah was coming from. Thoughts in her mind were running with the same crazy rush, as she was: "Finally, he's coming, will I see him? Will the king allow him to see me? Or, is this the reason of his coming? I don't think so, he has thirty men with him, and the king would have to let them meet their families as well.,Oh!!!" She didn't realize whether these were just thoughts, or her mouth had whispered them out. She got herself together, and heard Azubah speaking as she was running after her:

"My Bath-Sheba, don't think now, time will show what the future will bring; think of this, when we come back home."

Now they were near the main street, which was full of people. Everyone running, staggering, and getting up, children crying, laughing, and taking dust with their hands, and throwing it up in the air with joy. At last, they found a spot where they could see them coming. So many eyes were seeking to find their wistful love. The men on the horses had their eyes upon the crowd as well, and in the midst of those eyes made fierce by war, but softened by longing, she found his. But now, now she couldn't look at those eyes that she had dreamed of, and impatiently waited for. She put her head down and tried to hide the tears that were falling down her cheeks. She knew, more than tears of longing, those were tears of guilt, a guilt that she was carrying like a stone in her soul, ever since the king had made her, his. She felt Azubah's hand holding her, and her feet wearing out of strength. She raised her head a little, and saw that they had moved on, but his eyes were still looking back to find hers, and she didn't have the courage to lift them up.

"Azubah," she murmured. "I can't anymore. Let us get back home."

"Bath-Sheba, they're entering the palace now, of course, we shall return."

For the first time she noticed that the crowd had pushed them all the way near the palace. Something made her look up at the terrace. And there he was, frozen and overwhelmed in thoughts, he: her love, her promise, the king. She felt her body fill with tremor, and her soul with a feeling that he alone had given. But the guilt didn't hinder to remind her that now her only rescuer was Uriah.

***

They started to get back home. Serenity was returning in the streets and everywhere. As they were walking, she saw a little girl drawing on the ground, just like she had, when a little kid. She stopped and looked, and saw that it was the same sun that she used to draw when she was little, but instead of rays it had tears. She sat by the little girl's side and asked her:

"Why is the sun crying?"

"It is not crying. It is a newborn and its rays haven't formed yet, that's why it looks like it is crying. When it grows up, the tears will hold on to each other and will become rays, and then this will be a big sun. It's still little," the little girl explained. "This will be the king of all suns and all stars."

Bath-Sheba smiled, caressed her hair and got up. But the little girl held her by the hand and said:

"Wait, I want to show you how my sun will become king. Here, see!"

She sat hastily and started drawing lines, putting the drops together. Bath-Sheba froze as she saw the Star of David around the circle that looked like a sun. Her eyes that were still tearful, smiled to hide the anguish that she held inside, and with a voice that pretended to be happy, she spoke and at the same time walked away:

"That is beautiful, little girl!"

***

As they approached the house, Azubah walked ahead to open the door for Bath-Sheba who was feeling weak and frail. She got in, took the kerchief off her head and immediately put her hands on her tummy, as if that unborn creature was crying, just like she was. She patted it softly and spoke gently:

"Don't cry my sweet-heart, I have been waiting for you for so long, and now here you are. Uriah didn't bring you to me, but someone who changed my life completely. It is not your fault. Life is not at fault, neither is love. It is I who made a mistake, with my adultery." And she started sobbing.

Azubah, quickly closed the door and went near her, embraced her and said: "No my daughter, not again. Please it is not right to speak of sin and forgiveness now. Please calm down. Let the child grow in peace inside you, and don't put on him a burden that only your soul should carry. I'll show you something that you don't know, but first you have to calm down."

***

She became speechless and with a curiosity that couldn't wait to hear Azubah's secret, she put her eyes on her and waited patiently. She asked herself: "How can Azubah have a secret? She's been with me ever since I can remember! What could it be?"

"I was very close with your mother, long time before you were born, we were best friends. "She started to speak. "If it weren't for her wish, I would have never been your nanny. She and I grew up together, we did everything together, and even when she would do something wrong, she would come to me and pour out her heart. My father was a carpenter, and we would always go in his workshop to play in the middle of wood chips and boards. Once, she took a piece of wood and started to carve it, she filed it little by little and gave it a heart shape. One day she gave it to me and told me:

'This is my heart. When I am no more, make it live for me!'

I felt a piercing in my chest, but I laughed and said:

'What are you saying? Stupid!'

Nevertheless, I took that heart, and here I still have it".

She got up from where she was and went into her room. Opened an old wooden chest and took out that piece of wood in the shape of a heart that was given to her long time ago.

Without giving Bath-Sheba a chance to speak, she continued: "When she gave birth to you, I was there. She was very tired from the labor, sweat had covered her completely, and chills were shaking her body. But you, she didn't want to have you off her bosom. She kept you there, looking into your eyes and speaking words that only she could:

'I will call you Bath-Sheba, I will call you love, I will call you purity, I will call you blessed, and I will call you mother of the king, because I am the mother of the queen. You are my queen, my daughter!'

I was beside her and it seemed like, with those words and blessings that she was saying, she was putting a royal crown on your little head. You would look into her eyes, with those half-opened eyes of yours, with colors that changed every moment, and you would move your hands in every direction as if you wanted to catch not only every sound coming out of her mouth, but all the love that had filled the room. As she was looking how lively you were, and as sweat was still covering her, she said to me:

'Azubah, do you still have that heart that I gave you when we were little?'

I looked at her in wonder and I answered:

'Of course I still have it!' She became calmer, and she spoke again:

'Please bring it to me, I want to say something!'

When I gave it to her, she passed her hand on it softly, as if it really were her heart, and whispered in her fatigue:

'I don't know if I'll see my little Bath-Sheba grow up, I don't know if I'll be able to teach her how to make embroidery, how to cook, how to wash...'

She spoke with tears in her eyes, and a bitter smile wandered on her lips.

'I feel I will leave soon, but one thing comforts me: I know my daughter is going to be more than a woman, she will become more than a mother; she will be the mother of a king. She will be blessed with a love that blessed me and made me a mother, her mother. Please, dear Azubah, raise her and do what I will not be able to do. When you see her become a mother, give this heart to her!' "

***

Bath-Sheba wasn't crying anymore, but she was confounded as she was keeping that wooden heart in her hands. She was trying to find a reason for all that was happening in her life. How could everything be good, and so wrong? She got up and went by the window, keeping the heart in her hands, and looked up at the terrace. She saw the king standing there immobile as if he had been that way since the soldiers had come. She placed the heart on her tummy, and spoke as if her mother was there, in front of her:

"Here is the king's child, mother, here is the child that is making me a queen, the child that is suffering from my adultery!" She put the heart up on the window and continued:

"And there is the king. Now I'm waiting for salvation, I'm waiting for life!"

The meeting with the king was now over, and he had given them permission to go and spend time with their families. They were all looking at Uriah, who was standing silent in one of the corridors in the palace, trying to do more than thinking. He was having these struggling thoughts on the king's kindness and words:

"I know your bravery, your fight; I know the commitment you have toward our people. I also know that you've been away from your families, your wives, children; away from the ones who love you and are your support here. It is a small gift of gratitude that I want to offer you for your service and loyalty toward the king, and the people, that I allow you to spend this night in your homes."

These words gave him a responsibility that was different from the one he bore in war. He had to make a decision not for victory in battle, but for the pleasure of the soul and for the desire of the longing that had burned their hearts ever since they had left. With these thoughts in his mind, he started walking toward the palace door, to go out in the courtyard where the tents had been put up for them. He started to feel once again the same doubt that he had felt during the night, and he didn't know how to escape from it. He turned his head, and noticed his friends were behind him, like saying that no matter what his decision, they would support him all the way. He entered in his tent and for a moment he thought he heard Bath-Sheba's voice saying:

"I'm waiting for you, I miss you, I want to live loving you again!"

He was shaken by that thought, and saw that Ira, one of his closest friends, had come in the tent behind him. He spoke to Uriah as if he had heard the thought that had troubled him:

"Uriah, the king is honoring us, it is even a miracle that he is allowing us to spend time with our families. But this permission should not be a torture for us; it should be something that we'll do without fear in our hearts. Give your decision and don't doubt in it."

He looked at him straight in the eyes trying to find not only support, but also an answer.

"Ira, you know me well. Of course I feel honored, and also humbled by the king's words. But I have this doubt in my heart. You know my love for Bath-Sheba, you know my commitment toward her, but how can I go into my house, knowing that our army is in open field ready for war? How can I enter my doorstep to embrace my life's love, knowing that the Ark of the Lord is in a tent? How can I eat or drink from Bath-Sheba's hands, knowing that our people are hungry for victory? As it is true that the king lives," he changed his tone, setting aside all uncertainty, "I will not do this."

Saying these words he and Ira got out off the tent to speak to the other men, who were outside, but to their surprise they all shouted in one voice:

"Amen!"

The burden he had inside got lighter from that word, and he sent word to the king with one of the palace's guards.

***

He got inside the tent again and heard a laughter that startled him. He turned his head around to see where it came from, and saw that somewhere behind the covers something that was moving. He got near and at the same time moved back, when a little girl jumped in front of him holding out her hand with something in it.

"Who are you? Do you know you shouldn't be here?"

"I am Tamara, the king's daughter. I have done embroidery for you, because I know you are the strongest of all."

He looked in her eyes that were shining from joy, and caressed her gently, while she opened her hand. She had embroidered the king's star on a small red piece of linen with a yellow, shining thread. She took his big strong hand, and opening his fingers one by one, she placed the embroidery there saying:

"See, your hand is a fighter's hand."

Saying this, she ran quickly outside leaving Uriah astounded.

"You didn't give me a chance to thank you little girl, not even tell you that all king's soldiers are as brave!"

***

With these unsaid words, he got out of the tent, not to enter there again for that afternoon. Even though the day hadn't been very busy, it had given him enough fatigue, worries and doubts that had dried up his soul. He was holding the embroidery in his hand and was thinking of that little girl that had praised him with her childish way. Two words came into his mind: "Child of the king!" and though he didn't know what meaning they held, they gave some warmth to his heart. A hand patted his shoulders; he turned his head and greeted Ira who was standing behind him.

"Uriah, you didn't sleep all night, last night, go lay down to rest, I'll do the thinking tonight."

He smiled and said:

"Yes, but you won't be thinking of Bath-Sheba, but Rachel and your little Benjamin. Did you see them running after you, yesterday, when we arrived in the city?"

"I've never been touched by her voice like yesterday, and never before have I wanted to play with my son, like I wanted yesterday. I don't know how I didn't get off the horse, may be because I thought I was off the horse, I felt like I was hugging them both with the greatest strength that God had given me. Ah, Uriah, sometimes I get so confused with this love I have inside."

"No, Ira," interrupted Uriah as he was tossing and turning Tamara's embroidery in his hands, " We have a promise that we have to give to our people and this promise will be given to us only if we fight for it."

***

They got silent and started to walk in the yard, which seemed to be surrounded not by walls, but by vastness. In silence all night, each of them thought of their longing and love. The morning had come again inviting them for yet another meeting with the king, where he would give his instructions and guidance before they left. After they cleansed and had breakfast the servant of the king directed them to the salon.

***

Uriah was looking down at the stars sculptured on the floor, and in his hand he was holding tight the embroidery that the little girl had given him the day before, which, surprisingly, had given him peace, after the qualm he had experienced. He thought of her, he also thought of Bath-Sheba, thought of their future together. He had nephews and nieces, but never had he thought of the love he would have as a parent, as he thought when this little girl gave him this embroidery. He recalled a conversation he had had with Bath-Sheba in the beginning of their life together: "How I desire to be a parent with you, how I want to raise children with you, how I wish for you to be the mother of my children, to raise them and bless them with the beauty and goodness of your soul!" And she answered back: "Our children will be happy, because you will be their father, they will play with you, will run with you, will be spoiled by you, will learn what true love is from you, they will be children of a fighter!"

***

The king was waiting sitting on his throne with a face where he was trying to hide his disappointment.

"My men, I am proud of you, but also a little disappointed that you didn't accept my gift. Didn't you come from a long and tiring way? Aren't you giving glory to the army of Israel? Why then, didn't you go into your homes?"

Uriah came forward again and humbly started to speak slowly, but with determination.

"My lord, I and the servants of your majesty, didn't deny your gift, on the contrary, that is an honor for us. But how could we embrace our families, how could we be served from our women, when the Ark of the Lord and Israel are in the battlefield? If we would really take advantage of your goodness, o king, we wouldn't be worthy of fighting for you."

8

The king stood still. How strange! These very words he had said so many times to himself, when he had been in war with his army, but now they had no meaning. This man, a simple officer in his army, with his attitude was speaking to his conscience, while his mind was almost screaming: "You should give yourself to your wife Uriah; you should become the father of the child she's carrying!"

He got up from his throne trying to calm those cries and spoke to the soldiers that were standing before him.

"Since this day, today, is your last day, I am throwing dinner revelry for you, which will start in the evening, after the sunset. I want to once again thank you for your service, and also I want to point out that your faithfulness has touched me, and I'm grateful for your fight. You may leave."

He greeted with his head and walked away toward the terrace, which had become a refuge from the present. The only hope he had left, was that this dinner event, would change Uriah's mind, and make him one with his wife.

***

Even though the corridor was noisy, like usual, to him it felt like time had stopped and had covered the palace with a deadly silence. He walked and remembered Saul, remembered his persecution, his jealousy, his decision to kill him. He recalled how Jonathan, his heart's friend, had interfered to his father and had said:

"My king, father, don't sin against your servant, David? Haven't his deeds been worthy of your kingdom, has he committed any wrong against you? He risked his life when he killed Goliath. The Lord delivered us through David. You saw it, and you rejoiced; why sin against innocent blood, why kill David without a cause?"

Saul regarded his son's words and swore not to do wrong to David. He even invited him in his tent for supper. David had gone to Saul and had offered him his service again, but Saul never understood David's commitment. Filled with jealousy again and in his passion to kill David he had thrown his arrow toward him, as he was playing the harp to the king's satisfaction.

***

David was scared of this memory, but justified himself without even believing that justification, that he was doing everything for Bath-Sheba, for the love he had for her and the child that was growing inside her. And as he tried to comfort himself as little as possible in his deeds, he saw his little girl, Tamara, who had followed him and was asking for his attention:

"My girl, you are so sweet!"

"Father, please. Tell me Abraham's story."

He hugged her and started to tell her one of the stories that his mother had told him when he was little like Tamara.

"Abraham was very old when God made him father," he started speaking. "He had a joy in his heart that can't be told in words. He lived with this joy everyday as he saw his son growing up.

Later he had another son. He loved them both so endlessly. They played together, slept together, learned from each-other and loved each-other dearly. Abraham was happy, because God had kept his promise, when He had told him that his descendants would be as many as the sand by the sea, as the stars in a clear night sky. But one day God spoke to him and told him to send away his older son and his mother. Abraham was saddened deeply by this, but nevertheless, he obeyed to God's command and prepared the child and his mother to be sent away. He put them on a mule, gave them food and water and, with the hope that their journey would take them in a secure place gave them his blessing to go. The boy was crying, and the little one also couldn't bear the separation and ran after his brother crying. Abraham dashed after his little boy, embraced him tightly and said:

'Don't worry, I'm sending him there, where God has a big promise for him.' And the little boy answered:

'But there is promise here too, why not have him here?' And Abraham spoke with pain in his voice:

'Because this promise here belongs only to you. None can have your promise, but you!'

The boy remained crying in his father's arms till he fell asleep. Abraham took him to his covers and lay with him. As he was by his son, he heard God's presence and, with a voice that was still struggling from the pain of separation spoke:

'Lord, is it you? Tell me what you want?' and the Lord answered:

'Take Isaac, your only son, and go to the top of the mountain to offer him as a sacrifice to me!'

Hearing these words, Abraham got up in terror and felt as if God stopped existing. In his heart he had this unbearable fight: his love for his son and his obedience toward God were scuffling with each-other. And at last, the hope that God would resurrect the little boy after he had been offered as a sacrifice, won! Obedient and in pain, he left from where his son was sleeping, and went to notify the servants to get ready for journey the next day. The place where he had to make his sacrifice was a few days walk, so they had to take food, water and covers, and wood for the fire of sacrifice. The day dawned to Abraham's disappointment, who had hoped to die before sacrificing his son, and together with his servants and his son, who was so happy and laughing in his unawareness, took the road. When they got at the edge of the mountain, Abraham told his servants to remain there, and took the woods for the fire, and his son, and started climbing. The boy saw that his father hadn't taken the sacrifice and asked:

'Father, did you forget to take the lamb for the sacrifice?' As if the weight of the wood weren't enough, this question made Abraham wearier, and trying to hold his tears that had become a knot in his throat, he answered:

'Son, God will provide the sacrifice!'

They walked, and walked, and when they got at the top of the mountain, Abraham asked his son to help him set up the altar where they would put the sacrifice, and once they had set it up, he put his son on and started to tie him up silently. The boy was standing still, completely trusting what his father was doing, and even when Abraham took the knife, and with a sobbing spirit lifted it up to pierce his son's heart, he didn't move, neither doubted his father's action. In that moment, the earth shook and the boy felt the ropes break, while the knife fell off of Abraham's hands, and a voice stronger than thunder spoke:

'Abraham, Abraham!'

Abraham spoke with a voice trembling with fear:

'Here I am!'

Then the voice became softer, as if it too, was living the same pain that Abraham was:

'Do not lay your hand on the boy, do not cause him any harm. Now I know that you fear God, because you have not withheld your only son from me.' "

David stopped speaking and put his hand on Tamara's head, who was now sleeping on his lap. A tear fell from his eyes and woke the little girl, who raised her head and spoke whispering in her sleep:

"Father, isn't it true that God asks only of those who are faithful and ready to sacrifice, and not of those who disobey and do not listen to His Voice?"

She rubbed her still shining eyes, and got up without taking any answer from her father, as if she had already given it in her question. She kissed her father on the cheek and went to her room, without noticing her father's eyes that were in tears.

***

He stood there thinking of Abraham and the words that his daughter said as she left. He felt that he had fallen away from every promise, and had taken upon himself something that he had never had before: his life. Meanwhile, he remembered that it was almost evening and he had to prepare for dinner with his soldiers. The feeling of guilt disappeared from that moment that was promising to solve every problem, and give life to his love. He got up and went to his room to get ready, with a determined hope that everything should end that very night.

***

The tables were ready, the musicians were playing their instruments, and the soldiers were eating and drinking as if they would never go back to war. The king had ordered for the best wine and had asked the best cook to prepare the best foods, with the hope that the wine and the food would take Uriah to his wife. Noise filled the salon; the palace was overflowed with laughter like never before. Some dancers made their way in the salon, and the musicians started playing royal music. The soldiers, who were satisfied with food and wine, started singing, but Uriah stood still at the table.

It was the peak of pleasure of that evening, when the king got up, and as he had made it a custom, took his harp and started to sing.

"May the Lord answer you on your day of need
May the Name of God of Jacob protect you from above
May He send you help from His Holy Place
May He sustain you from Zion
May He never forget your offerings
And may He be pleased with your sacrifice
May He give you your heart's desires
May He guide you with His counsel."

He finished his song, got up, put the harp on the stool, and walked toward Uriah. Approached him and spoke with a voice that tried to hide itself in the noise that had started to fill the room again:

"Uriah, I see that the pleasure of wine and food has captured your hearts. If you want to share this joy with your wives, you have my blessing to go, and present yourselves before me in the morning, before you leave."

Though drunk with the satisfaction of this majestic evening, Uriah didn't forget his zeal and determination which made him say again:

"As it is true that my lord, my king lives, as it is true that your soul lives, so it is true that I will not put foot in my house."

Though caught in songs and excitement, the soldiers answered in a solid "Amen" that surprised not only Uriah, but the king too, who felt his heart break together with the last hope that he had left.

***

He walked toward his table, sat and stayed there till the last servant had finished cleaning up the room. Stuck in his mind were the drunk, but firm words of Uriah that took away the hope of saving Bath-Sheba and the unborn child. Finally his fear had become an inevitable deed he had to act upon. He realized he couldn't give him to his wife, so in his mind he decided to give him to his enemies, to the enemies of his kingdom. But how could he do this? None better than him knew how it is to fight, to be persecuted, to live in the mercy of those who have no heart, and who only know how to kill. Nevertheless, he was giving an innocent man to pay for his own guilt; he was giving him to death, so that he could have everything that man had ever owned: his wife, his love.

***

Drowned in the mud of his own soul, he went to his room, took a piece of paper and started writing with a shaking culpable hand to Joab, the commander of his army: "Set Uriah in the forefront of the hottest battle, and retreat from him. You understand why…. that he may be struck down and die."

It was him, David, the one who had fought and killed Goliath, the most horrendous enemy of Israel who was hiding his life behind a man who was guilty only of his bravery. He, the king, who had been blessed with everything he had ever wanted, was stealing from a man the only gift he had, other than his life, his wife. But how could he establish the justice he himself had violated in the passion of a fiery love? Every transgression requires an offering of redemption, and he could give anything, but his life, which he wanted to bury together with that breathtaking moment, in the death of a committed brave man. Drenched in a torment that was crumbling his bones, sunk in his shame, he awaited anxiously the offering of an undeserved sacrifice.

9

It was an early smiling morning, and Uriah woke up with a word that he had heard from the king a long time ago: "The mercies of the Lord are new every morning!" Though his head was heavy from the drinking of the night before, he got up and saw his friends were ready to present themselves before the king. He dressed up quickly, ran to the other side of the court where the basins were for cleansing, washed, and even though breakfast was ready, he didn't feel like eating, but said:

"Ready to go, then. Let's take the king's blessing."

It was early and the palace was quiet. The cicadas were still singing in a night that was fainting under the sunny rays that were shining stronger as the day broke. They entered the salon and Uriah stood before the king, as he started speaking:

"Men, I wish you victory and may God guard your lives, just like you are guarding the promise given to our people. Uriah, I want you to give this letter to Joab and tell him to follow my instructions in every detail."

He extended his hand to take the letter, but suddenly, it fell from the king's hands, which seemed to be a little shaky. He bowed down and it felt as if that letter was really heavy and Uriah's hands shivered with a responsibility he had never faced before.

"You may depart with my blessing," continued the king, and gestured for them to leave.

***

They exited the palace leaving behind the gate that was closing, but now the city ahead of them was empty. What were left of the noise that awaited them when they came, were its echoes and memories. Somewhere at a corner, Bath-Sheba's and Azubah's images were standing frozen, and on the street still remained undamaged Rachel's footsteps as she had ran with little Benjamin in her arms, calling Ira. The street wasn't lively anymore, nor was it quiet; it echoed a silenced sent off, as if it echoed death.

***

They arrived at the camping place where the army had set up the tents, and Uriah left his friends and went to meet with Joab to give him the king's letter. He was walking through the tents that were swarming with noise and laughter. Someone came out of a tent and spoke in a friendly way:

"Uriah, you're back," he said as he drew near with an embrace and shook his hand.

"Yes, yes. How's everything going here?" said Uriah, as he embraced him back.

"We've surrounded the city, and the Ammonites have started their retreat, but we have not been able to progress our offensive at their gates. They have put many of their bravest men, and the fight has been fierce. We've had great loss, but God is giving us heart with the promise of victory, which will soon be ours."

"Yes, brother, it is so. Let's not forget that we're here to take the promise given to our people and our families.... Now I have to meet with Joab."

***

They embraced and went their own way. Uriah walked, heard, thought, and spoke to himself: "How strange it feels that I'm here again, indeed it feels like I never left, like I never felt any doubt, like I never saw Bath-Sheba cry or shiver! It looks like time has stopped here assigning me more than just a fight." He realized he had taken off his chest the embroidery of the star that the little girl had given him. He was holding it in his hands and looking it thoughtfully. For a moment he thought it was the very sun that Bath-Sheba used to draw when they were children, a star-sun with infinity inside. He touched it gently with the warm memory he found in his heart, and put it back in his chest again.

***

He got at the commander's tent and asked to be announced.

Joab was a brave man of Israel, but had used his bravery, not rarely, for his selfish and arrogant reasons. He had killed many people and most of them in peaceful times. His bravery was known, probably more because of the fear he had sowed through his wickedness, treachery, and his barbarism. He never valued friends or enemies, but nevertheless, the king had always rewarded this man with his trust by keeping him commander of his army.

In the mean time the guard allowed him to go in as he opened the curtain of the tent. He entered slowly, as if he was entering a forbidden place and waited for Joab. Two candle holders were put at the corners of the tent, and were shining its darkness. There was a table in the middle with maps and charts, and there were a few old stools around it; further back down at the corner there were put some big pillows, and from behind a curtain that divided the tent in two, out came Joab. He greeted with a cold salutation and asked Uriah to sit on one of the stools around the table.

"Welcome back Uriah. How did the meeting with the king go? Did he give any instructions for me?"

"Thank you my lord. The meeting went well, and the king was very interested for our advancement, for the well-being of this army, and your health. After he heard our report, he gave me this letter for you."

He was giving him the letter, and it fell off his hand as if it was carrying an invisible weight. He picked it up and handed it to Joab. He opened it quickly and started reading it mutely. Uriah was trying to read the king's words, directions, and guidance in Joab's lifeless eyes. But all he understood was the emptiness of this big man that was standing in front of him, this man with little white hair, coarse hands, and with a heart that had probably stopped beating a long time ago. He got up, thanked Uriah and said:

"Tomorrow we'll start with our major offensive. The sons of Ammon are determined at the city's gates and have barred us from entering, but we'll strike them there with all our strength. You will take your men, and together with the men of Heleb, the son of Baanah, will go at the dawn of the day to prepare the battlefield in front of the city's gates. You will attack them unexpectedly, and then I will follow with the rest of the army to enter the city after you. God be with you, my son! You may go."

For the first time Uriah sensed a little warmth in the words of this man, whose aloofness was felt throughout the entire camp.

***

Uriah departed in obedience, and went toward the tent where his men had been set up. They were cleansed, and were resting. He sat near Ira and spoke so that all could hear:

"Tomorrow we have a big day ahead of us. Joab just informed me that we'll start one of our fiercest endeavors. The Ammonites have blocked us at the city's gates, and we'll be in the front line to open the way for our army. Heleb and his men will be with us, too. We'll start before the dawn, I even say, we should position ourselves tonight, so that their guards may not see us."

They were all calm, as he was speaking. It felt as if the silence of the city that they had left behind had dressed up their boldness to prepare them for the coming fight. They got up wordlessly and without expecting any specific order started to get ready. They knew what the order was: "Charge!"

***

They had been fighting for a few days. The fight became more violent by the moment. Some of them had gone back to the camp wounded; some had stayed even though their body was pierced by the enemy's sword. Uriah had positioned himself near the main gate, and Ira with a few more men was with him. They fought with their heart and soul, with longing and desire, with love and hatred. Uriah's sword swayed in the air like an eagle chasing its prey, but not too long and he realized he had gone far from his men, and found himself in the middle of enemies who with their swords didn't spare his body. He didn't feel any pain until he saw the embroidery come out of his chest, hanging on the tip of a sword that penetrated his heart. He extended his hand to grab it, and held it tightly with the very last strength that he still had. He felt his heart speak with a slow beat, as if it was saying:

"A lonely star was left in the sky
Without a gleam
Without a beam
And tired as it was it fell from the stream
To come and rest in your singing dream."

He closed his eyes, and holding the little girl's embroidery in his fist, felt departing somewhere, in a place of promise and victory.

10

David was sitting on the throne and waiting for the courier to give him news from the battlefield. A strange fear had taken hold of his heart for days. He signaled with his hand and waited worriedly for the news.

"My lord, I come today to say to you that yesterday was a day of loss for our army. Our insistent attack at the city's gates was repelled by brave men of Ammon. Many were wounded and some killed..."

"Why would Joab show such zeal and not consider the lives of our soldiers?" He interrupted in distress that made him yell and get off his throne.

"My lord," spoke the courier with a voice that was drowning inside him, "your servant Uriah the Hittite is dead, also."

The king was appalled by this news that dimmed his strength, as if the sword that pierced Uriah's body was now going through his soul. He sat and didn't speak anymore.

***

One of the councilmen allowed the courier to leave. The salon became empty, and the king was left alone with the betrayal that was slaying his heart. He pulled his hair, pounded his chest with despair, and laid on the ground as if it would get him near the one who had given his life for him. He put his hands on the tiles and touched every detail sculpted on them with his fingers, and with the eyes that had gotten dark from this torturing pain, he saw his star. He picked up the robe that had fallen down, got up, and remembered his daughter's embroidery. That man was his hero, his redeemer, the carrier of his star.

***

He came out of the salon with the pain that sunk inside him, and advised one of the guards to take the news to Bath-Sheba; meanwhile he walked to his room. He went near the window and stayed there for a moment. His heart shivered for her, he groaned for her fear, her longing, and her loss. He realized how his love, his sin, had given her more than an affair in darkness; he had given her grief. In his mind he still heard the courier's words, which became one with words written in the Law, in that Law that made him hide himself, and offer the sacrifice. "If someone is caught… kill… many of ours… they should be punished…" And now, the Law reminded him not only of his betrayal, but also his murder, the murder he committed with the hand of that betrayal. "If a man acts with premeditation against his neighbor to kill him with guile, you shall take him from my altar that he may die." Yet again, the Law, stronger than his transgression, igniting an accusatory anger inside him, that didn't blame him, but the Law itself.

"O, I wish that you didn't exist, that you were never written, that God had created the universe lawless, and that my love didn't deceive, didn't kill, was not punished… I blame you, not myself; I blame you because your existence is my punishment, a punishment that I don't deserve, a punishment that shouldn't haunt me, a punishment that…that will kill my love. O Lord, I wish you had interfered, that you didn't allow the deception and the killing, and that you let me love without laws, without punishment. O Lord, it is too late now, my hand has intruded where you should have and now, there is nothing left, but her, my Bath-Sheba, my love, my adultery, my murder, to be with me, and her life to take away this bitterness…"

***

As he tried to blame the one he had obeyed and followed all his life, the one who had made him a worrier, the one who made him king, as he tried to blame the Lord for his Law, for that Law that sustains the heavens and the earth, the stars and the sun, His Star, he noticed the guard and the courier knock on Bath-Sheba's door. He trembled, and forgot the Lord, just as he had forgotten Him all this time, and felt that knock beat his heart that stopped pounding. What would she do? Would she open the door, or her nanny? Would she blame him, or would she mourn to forget Uriah, and become his forever?

"Bath-Sheba, I wish you didn't have to hear this news today, oh how I wish that you didn't have to hear it today, or tomorrow, or ever. Ah, I wish you didn't have to listen, didn't have to understand, just for today, oh… what can I do so that this news doesn't come to you? It seems like this is a very long knock, it's like a sword standing on me, waiting to cut me, to pierce me, cut me in pieces, give me suffering, but not death."

He withdrew from the window leaving there his fear of self, his love, his fall, and strayed in his sin, far from God, he remembered psalms that he had sang to Him:

"You are the rock of my salvation, o Lord
You are the strength of my life.
Lord, you are my light.
And you are my hope and inspiration."

Had he lied to himself with a false faith, had he fought all his life with a bravery that his pride had given him, was love that he had for God not real love, but a passion which he was now putting to death with a killing anger? Doubts and questions were raiding his soul:

"But the anointing, I was chosen... were those lies, too? If the Lord knows my ways, He should have known this? Why did he let me do this, why am I in this isolation, why am I king? Why am I not a shepherd any more? I would never doubt my faith, I would never disappoint my love, I would never be angry with God, and I would never betray His Law. Why did He forsake me?"

***

These doubts and questions plowed sobbing in his soul, which couldn't find consolation anywhere. He had stepped on himself, he had shamed his anointing. How could he find forgiveness for himself, how could he find forgiveness in God? Emptiness was now his new song, sorrow was his loneliness, and forgetfulness was his hiding place.

Vanity of vanities, this was now his season, the season where past would be his accuser, his judge, and his punisher.

11

She woke up terrified from a dream that had made her scream. Azubah ran near her and stroke her sweated face with caresses.

"Praise God!" said Bath-Sheba when she realized she'd been dreaming.

"Tell me, what's wrong, my daughter?"

"Azubah, I had a dream, not a bad dream, but I don't know why I got so scared. Let me think... I dreamt that I was with Uriah laid in a field of daisies. Then I got up and walked till I found a place where I could draw; I started drawing on the ground with my finger a sun, like the one that little girl was drawing when Uriah came. I drew the circle and then the tears, and at this moment Uriah came near and sat by me; he started drawing lines that joined the tears together, and the sun became like that little girl's: The Star of the King. Then he took the piece of ground with his hand, and it became like embroidery; his hand started bleeding from something in the dust, and the embroidery became red, while the star remained yellow. He looked me in the eyes and said:

'This is for you. Now I have to leave so that you may become the one you were born to be.'

He started running and I ran after him crying:

'Don't go, don't go!'

But he became one with the field and I was left alone with the embroidery in my hand. Then I started weeping in fear, because I was alone."

She looked around and cried again:

"Oh, no, this is a horrible dream. What if something happened to Uriah?"

Azubah embraced her and said:

"Stay calm, I'll bring you some honey that you may forget and sweeten your soul. Let this dream, be a dream and don't be troubled about it. You should think of the child, not dreams. Get up, now, cleanse yourself, and let the dreams die with the night, you should live with the day."

***

Bath-Sheba put her hand on her belly and started touching it softly, to take from there the security, and for the first time she felt a movement: a movement of life, goodness, and love; a movement that brought a smile on her lips and a new feeling in her heart: "Good morning to you, too! I am your mommy!" she spoke to that movement. "And who are you? Are you my son, or my daughter?" She kept her hand on her tummy as she felt life make her face glow and the room brighten.

***

Someone was knocking on the door, and she laughed at Azubah who tripped while running to open it. Azubah looked at her smiling, and opened the door that was shaking from the hard knock. Bath-Sheba looked from behind her, to see who it was, and remained frozen with a face where the night's dreadfulness had returned again. She came near the door and stood beside Azubah to hear what the king's courier had to say, but he was standing speechless in front of them.

"My lord, tell us, what is it?" demanded Azubah as she saw the courier's silent face, who continued to stay immobile and wordless in front of these two women as if he were afraid of them.

Bath-Sheba worried even more, when she noticed his quivering hands as they were holding embroidery, where the blood had left its mark. She screamed and fell numb on the floor. Azubah turned quickly, and called at the men who were still wordless in front of the door:

"Move, come inside and help me put her in her covers."

She tried to remain calm as she sensed the horrid news which remained untold in the mouths of these muted men. As she tried to hold back her tears, and put Bath-Sheba in her covers, she asked the men once again to speak.

"Tell me, tell me, what has happened to my lord? Tell me!"

"He's been killed."

These were the only words told, and Azubah burst in tears that made Bath-Sheba sentient again.

***

She let the men go, and remained wooden in this bereavement that the day had brought. She felt something like a bitter liquid run from her chest to her stomach, and she put her hands on her tummy as if that would prevent that bitterness from going there. Tears like heavy rain streamed on her cheeks, while her voice became sorrow underneath her breath. Her legs became sluggish again, while her body withered in Azubah's arms once more. Her wavy bosom smashed its waves on Azubah's gentle lap, while her being wobbled in memories of the past that found their rest on the shore of her heart.

***

He, her friend, her song, her love, her security, everything she had, was no more. All that was left of him was an embroidery stained with his blood, which the guard had handed to her before he left. She put it near her face, as if it were a flower which she wanted to water with the rain of her tears, and tried to find there as little scent of his life as possible. She kissed it softly, caressed it with her face, placed it near her heart and it felt as if that embroidery was talking to her with the song that he had once sang: "A lonely star was left in the sky....and tired as it was it fell from the stream...!" She set her clouded eyes on the star of the king and felt a whisper inside saying: "Farewell!"

She wept, and wept and cried out to the one who was no more. She called him because she loved him, because she needed his forgiveness. She called him to come back so that she could give him her life. Her love and desire had killed him and she wanted to give him life all over again with her sorrow and repentance. In the suffering of her two loves, she knew she was the only one that must lose. But, the child?

***

Her belly filled with a frightened joy, and she caressed it softly saying: "You, my child, the child of my transgression, innocence of my guilt, blessing of my curse, love of my sorrow, joy of my mourning, life of my loss, child of my king..." She was overwhelmed by sadness and couldn't finish saying how much she loved that child. She felt the need of resting in Azubah's lap, and stayed there with her lamentations, until weariness threw her inside herself to give her strength in the dawn of a new day, which would carry with it a season of loneliness and mourning.

***

And truly, that day left with the news that it had brought. Tomorrow came carrying other questions and doubts, another light, another life, another future. A future that seemed untouched by the past, unafraid of pain, filled with the same love that it hoped to find inside her.

She was sitting, dressed in black clothes that made her hair shine like sun rays in twilight, looking at Azubah as she was preparing the bread for the Shabbat. She had put the oil near the flower, and some crushed salt in a small plate of clay, while she was standing on her knees, and worked the dough that become whiter with every touch. She was pouring there all her strength, until it would become like a thin sheet, ready to bake.

As she saw her, and thought of her life, being pressed just like that dough, she heard a gentle knock on the door. She gestured to Azubah not to move, and got up to open the door. A little boy, with green eyes that seemed like a forest where you could get lost to find its beauty, with a face that radiated joy, and with dirty hands, holding a small oil dish spoke:

"Shabbat Shalom! My mother sent me for some oil for the bread. It's almost sundown and she can't go to the market."

"Shabbat Shalom!" She answered and laughed with the little boy, who had remained faithful to his mother's words. She turned toward Azubah, who was up by now, and was holding the oil dish in her hands.

"There you go my son, and tell your mother to not return it, because God will. Shabbat shalom!"

***

The little boy left walking carefully not to spill any of the oil that was given. Bath-Sheba saw him leaving till he became one with the road, and realized she hadn't been out of the house for days. The air touched her pale face, the wind made her hair move under the black head-kerchief, and her clothes became bright from the sun. She lifted up her eyes to the sky; which was getting gloomy. She thought she heard God speak from that fog of clouds that was filling the horizon: "The sky is over the clouds, the sun comes after the storm, and you will go through your season of mourning to see joy in its season." The baby inside her moved as if it heard those words. She went back inside and sat down to see Azubah preparing the bread. But the door knocked again, and this time, stronger than the first time.

"Don't move my dear," said Azubah, and got up to open the door.

She was stunned seeing the king's servant standing there holding a letter in his hands.

"Come on in," she said looking around.

He entered, while Azubah closed the door.

"The king, my lord, has sent me to take Bath-Sheba in the palace. He requests that you become his wife. This letter is for you my lady."

She took the letter and opened it fast. She was staggered seeing that it was blank. She turned it back and forth, thinking that she wasn't looking it right, but the letter was white. She looked at the servant with a look that said: "Are you sure this letter is for me?" But he was as surprised as she was. She took Azubah aside and asked her:

"Azubah, what is this?"

She didn't say anything, but turned toward the servant and said:

"Please, say to my lord the king, he can send the guard to pick us up after the Shabbat."

She closed the door and squeezed Bath-Sheba with an embrace that made both of them tear. With the voice that was shaking she spoke sweetly.

"I didn't think that you had to suffer this much, I didn't think that love would take your life, but I know that your resurrection is near, God will make your light shine and your mourning will end."

She held her tightly till Bath-Sheba said laughing:

"Let go of me, you have dough on your hands!"

***

They laughed, but an excruciating pain pierced Bath-Sheba's back. She sat down to breathe and felt the child moving, and moving... Her tears of joy soon meddled with a regret that reminded her of her transgression.

"Azubah, I have dishonored God's Law. Who will die, so that I may live, who will hide my sin, who will take away my pain? This pain through my body, scares me, crushes me, it says to me: 'Everything must be washed; what should remain is only that moment when your love and the king's is not shame, is not sin, is not punishment!' I have sinned Azubah, I have sinned! Oh, that my sin is not my child!"

"Don't you cry my daughter, don't you cry," whispered Azubah, who was holding the same fear, the same trouble, the same uncertainty in her heart. But she prayed to the Lord with all her might so that He would forget the darkness and He would remember the love, and He would give His grace:

"O Lord, may your forgiveness be greater than your punishment, may your Hand be light on our sin, may your mercy be great upon this child, and may your love bury our transgression."

S he had come. The Shabbat was over and the guard had brought her
into the palace, where a room had been set up for her. She still was
in mourning, but he couldn't wait to see her. The night had fallen,
and the palace was quiet, he was walking toward her room, which was
at the end of the corridor. The candles were lit and his shadow followed
him in front and behind. He signaled the guard in front of her door to
leave, and entered.

She was still awake. Azubah was combing her hair, and when she
saw his shadow coming near, she walked away to live them alone.

"Bath-Sheba, I can't find any comforting words. The letter that I sent
was white, because I am wordless, but I wanted to show you that I was
there with you. I am voiceless because of your pain, I am deaf because of
your lamentation, I am faded because of your mourning, and I am dying
because of this anguish of love that has brought us here."

A tear sparkled on her eyelashes, and she wiped it with her hand.
She was now with him; she took his hand and put it on her belly. The
child was moving and David was moved from a happiness that he had
experienced many times before, but that always, felt new. He embraced
her and left without a kiss. He went to his room, where darkness wasn't
threatening, nor was the moonlight too strong, the stars were shining
cheerfully, and the sky was sleeping calmly in a night where everything
had been solved.

***

Her mourning was over and she now was his. He walked in the
corridors of the palace and every time he saw her, he felt comforted,
but something inside was still keeping buried a guilt that hadn't been
forgiven. Everything was over, but without an end, he had won, but the
outcome was loss. He had made his heart disobey his mind, and now was
asking it to put away the sadness.

Everyday came and went with its monotony: the courier came with news from war and he sent him back with guidance and advices, every evening he would check on Tamara and his other children, he took care of his wives, his servants and guards, but nothing filled the emptiness that his love, his deception, his murder had left in his heart: emptiness that could be only filled by God. But how? He couldn't face Him, he was angry at him, he had despised His Law, and he had departed from His Heart. David decided to wait till God Himself would forget, wipe out and forgive this sin.

***

He was now thinking of her moaning and pain, she was bringing forth life, was giving birth to the love they had shared. Azubah didn't let him inside the room, but in his hands he felt Bath-Sheba's sweat, in his mind he heard her thoughts, and in his body he felt her's and the baby's heart beat. When the baby came out, he heard Azubah shout joyously: "We have a son!" He didn't wait in the corridor, but went in the room and hugged Bath-Sheba, embraced Azubah tightly, and took in his hands the little boy, who was still unclean, but wrapped in a white sheet. His words were tears and laughters that filled the room. He placed the baby on Bath-Sheba's chest, and went away leaving a soft caress on her lips.

***

He reminisced when he first became a father. Amnon was his firstborn; he was his pride, the first being to call him: "father." He had felt like a child, amazed at the miracle of life, lost inside this marvelous gift of God: a child, life's continuance, promise of the future, eternity's face. That child had taught him the philosophy of life, had disclosed for him the mystery of self, which he had never known like that day. Life is long when you do what is right, and short when you run after vanity, totally exposed to God, and foreign to men, fearsome but beautiful for those who live in promise, dark and shadowy for those who have given their lives to selfishness. He had sung on that day like never before, and had praised God not only for the child, but also for his own life. He recalled that song, that song, that praise, and tears fell on his cheeks.

"Lord, you have searched me and known me;
You know my sitting down and my rising up;
You have hedged me behind and before

And laid your hand upon me
Your knowledge is too wonderful for me;
It is high, I cannot attain it.
I will praise you for I am fearfully and wonderfully made
Marvelous are your works
And my soul knows that very well.
My bones were not hidden from you
When I was made in secret
And wrought in the lowest parts of the earth
Your eyes saw my substance yet unformed
And in your book the days fashioned for me were written
And yet, there were none of them.
How precious are your thoughts to me o God
How great is the sum of them
All your works will praise you
I will rejoice in you and glorify you
I will lift up your name o creator of the universe
I will sing to you, who are the father of man
Who is but the dust of the earth
I will praise you o Most High.
I will declare your goodness every morning
And your faithfulness every evening
With a harp of ten strings, with my psaltery
And with the melody of my organ
Those who are planted in the house of the Lord
They will bloom in the gardens of our God.
They will give their fruit in their old days
They will be blossomed and green
To proclaim that the Lord is just, He is my shelter
And there is no injustice in Him
He gives me life, He gives me grace,
He is the only one worthy of praise
To you Creator of Universe, I sing!"

Now he had become father again, to live God's goodness, but this time, living it in transgression.

***

He started walking toward the salon with steps that were faster than his feet. The courier had come with news from war, and he sat on the throne with the happiness that the child had brought, and felt that happiness melt away as the courier spoke of failure and loss his army was encountering. His troubled council men gave their advice, while he stood unmoving in the middle of two worlds: happiness and sorrow, victory and failure, life and death; everything happening on the face of the earth, as if nothing interfered with anything.

***

The courier had just left and David was still standing on the throne with his hand on his chin, like Saul time ago, when he had told him he could conquer Goliath. Who was the Goliath of this war that was not ending? Was it his fault, his adultery, the murder he had committed? Would he find the strength to bring the bygone David back, the David that was blessed by his mother's heart, the David that was chosen after God's own heart, pull him out of the dark pit of sin, so that he would sing back the songs of victory, love, the songs of God's praises?

As he thoughtfully stood there, he heard steps approaching. He raised his head and saw the prophet of the Lord, Nathan, God's voice, coming toward him. His hair dusted by the wind, his noble face, his still walk, as if he was walking on water, his hands which held grace and forgiveness, spoke to him:

"My king, chosen of the Most High! I have come to tell you of an injustice that hasn't found judgment. There were two men in one city, one rich and the other poor. The rich man had exceedingly many flocks and herds, while the poor had nothing, but a little ewe lamb, which he had bought and nourished; he raised it with his children, giving it his own food, and quenching its thirst with his own cup, and holding it in his bosom to sleep. It was like a daughter to him.

A traveler came to the rich man's house, who didn't want to take from his own flock and herd to prepare one for the voyager; but he took the poor man's lamb and prepared it for the man that had come to him."

Overcome by sudden anger, the king got off his throne and said to Nathan:

"How can such unfairness take place in my kingdom? As is true that the Lord lives, this man deserves to die. He will restore fourfold for the lamb, because he had no pity. Who is this man?"

Silence had filled the salon, a silence that was only disrupted by the steps of the council men who were walking away, and the doors that were closing. Nathan, carrying a troublesome burden in his soul, spoke with a compassionate voice, like God's:

"You are that man, David. God is speaking to you and is reminding you that he has anointed you king, he gave you, Saul's, your master's house, and your master's wives into your arms, and He gave you the house of Israel and Judah, and if that had been too little, He would have given you more. Why, then, why have you despised God's word to do evil in His sight? You killed Uriah with the enemy's sword and you took his wife to be your wife. God will bring upon you the same adversity that you sowed; your wives will be taken from you before your eyes and be given to another who will lie with them during the day, and not night. What you did secretly, will be done to you before all Israel, before the sun."

Hit by a burning invisible slap, but that relieved him completely; the king fell on his knees, and with a voice that came from the depth of his heart said to Nathan:

"I have sinned against the Lord."

He couldn't speak anymore, but tears started writing repentance on his face, his lips like fall leaves suffering in sadness, his body aching, and his heart wounded from guilt, spoke to the only one who could hear him: "Forgive me o Lord, forgive me my Father, forgive me, forgive me!"

Nathan spoke again:

"The Lord has removed your sin, David. You will not die. However, because by this deed you have given great chance to the enemies of the Lord to blaspheme, the child that was born to you will become ill and will die."

Having said this, Nathan left, leaving the king laid on the floor, crying and sobbing. Plagued in waves of regret and sorrow, he heard the echo of the last words: "The child that was born to you will become ill and will die!" How could he make God overturn this decision? How could he save this infant, how could he stop this pain of loss that would cut Bath-Sheba's heart? He went to his room with anguish weighing over his shoulders, and spent the night there. He didn't answer to his servants' knocks, or to his children's cries, he didn't put any food in his mouth and let his body thaw, so that God would fill it with the salvation of his son's life. He remained laid on the floor, in repentance and curse, and prayed, and pledged with God so that He would show mercy to the child. He stood before Him and cried out to Him;

"Have mercy upon me, o God!
According to your loving-kindness
Blank out my transgressions!
Cleanse me thoroughly from my iniquity
And wash me from my sin.
For I acknowledge my wrongdoings
And my sin is ever before me
Against you and you alone have I sinned
And I have done what is evil in your eyes
Hide your face from my sins
And conceal my transgressions
Give me joy and gladness which only come from you
That the bones which you have broken may rejoice
Create in me a clean heart, o Lord
And do not take your Holy Spirit from me
Restore unto me the joy of your deliverance
And renew the right spirit within me!"

He wept and sobbed in sorrow, pleaded with hope that God would turn his shame in pride and his sadness in happiness. He asked in pain that He would keep Bath-Sheba and would spare her of her son's loss. He prayed to the Lord that He would forget the Law for the sake of life, for the sake of the child; he prayed that He would wash out his sin not with death, but with life.

***

A few days had passed by and the noise behind his door had died. He heard a few whispers and understood that now everything was really over. His love, sin, anger, repentance, was gone with the life of the infant. He got up, washed his red tired eyes from the tears, dressed up with clean clothes, ate, and set off to the House of the Lord. Walking toward that place that he had dedicated to God, he heard some of the servants who were startled with his behavior, saying: "He fasted and mourned when the child was still alive, and now that he's dead, he arouse and ate food!" He stopped and turned back speaking softly making everything and everyone silent:

"I fasted in hope and I mourned in hope. I thought the Lord would feel compassion in my sadness and grief, but his justice had to be put in place. The sin is mine, justice belongs to God; the child died because of me and I can't bring him back. I will go to him, but he can't come to me."

He continued his walk to the House of the Lord, and kneeled before Him giving his penitence, accepting His judgment, condemnation, and His forgiveness. With a crushed heart and a weary soul he spoke to the One that had given him life, anointing, and crowned him king. Humbled in repentance and tears, he felt his sin bury, and his spirit come alive again in God's forgiveness, and saw his first love resurrect, that love that he had given to God when in the fields as a shepherd, that love that his mother had nourished him with when a child.

He got up and signaled his guards to go ahead of him, and lifted up his eyes to the altar of the Lord and whispered:

"Praise and worship belong to you o God, to you who answers the prayer! My sins had overcome me, but you delivered me from my wickedness."

***

He walked toward the door and felt his whole being fill with the longing and love that he had kept away in the darkness where he had lived for so long. It was raining outside, a soft rain that moistened the dry ground, and spreading a fresh autumnal aroma in the air. The dust remained buried in the ground, while the wind blew bringing a new season, a season of forgetfulness and forgiveness. He entered the palace gates and saw life going on. The guards standing in their posts, the couriers coming and going, the officials running, the people waiting for the meeting time with the king to come, the children laughing and playing, everything seemed like an eternal painting. This colored his spirit with light and took away all obscurity. With the heart filled with life, he ran through the corridors to be near the woman he loved.

She was in black, enveloped in Azubah's arms, with eyes that didn't cry, but were filled with a hope that made the room gleam. With her silence she said:

"It is over! Now I wait a new beginning. The love we shared in darkness, now has come to light and it asks for your comfort and strength. We're not guilty anymore, we're forgiven!"

He walked to her and took her in his arms. He could feel her heart beating rapidly, her body shaking, her spirit waiting to come to life to fill the emptiness that darkness had left behind. He comforted her and gave her love again, a love that didn't suppress itself, wasn't ashamed, a love that was not afraid of light and didn't hide in the dark; a love that blessed them with its fruit and gave them a son.

***

It was a quiet evening. He was coming out of Tamara's room with a song in his mouth, and was headed towards Bath-Sheba's room to see the child that was born to them. As he drew nearer, he heard her voice speaking to the infant with a sweetness that only a mother's voice can have:

"One day, the Lord saw the most beautiful and the most shining star in the sky. He took it in his hand and brought it down on earth, and gave it to me. He put it in my tummy and one day that star came out of me in the form of a child. You are that child, you are, my precious Solomon!"

David felt his heart overwhelm with light and hope. He smiled and whispered gently:

"He will be called Solomon!"

Made in the USA
Charleston, SC
01 May 2013